I I IIIV
AIR

DISCARD

Library of Congress-in-publishing-data

Rubin, Charles
Leaning on Thin Air: A Novel of Boston, 1969/humor
1st Edition

Library of Congress Control Number: 2016908079
ISBN: 978-0-918915-07-8

Cover and text Design: Izumi Motai
Creative consultant: Jennifer Weil
Author photograph: Star Dewar

Printed in the United States of America
1st Edition
12345678910

NewCentury Publishers
PO Box 750265
Petaluma, CA 94975
Tel: 707 769 9808
Email: CRubin1244@aol.com
www.NewCenturyPublishers.com
Distributed by SCB Distributors/ Gardena, CA.

LEANING ON THIN AIR

A novel of Boston, 1969

CHARLES RUBIN

NEW
CENTURY
PUBLISHERS
Sonoma County, California

This book is lovingly dedicated to my sister, Irene Levy, and to my daughter, Pamela Jean Naugle

Acknowledgements

Remembering that long-ago generation
of daring, totally original copywriters and
art directors who stormed the bastions of
conventional, "let's fool the consumers"
advertising to create fresh, honest, innovative
and often hilarious TV and radio spots and
print campaigns. As forerunners of what has
become known as the Advertising Revolution,
their style, wit and inventiveness have often
been copied, but never equalled.

-1-

It's another Vietnam War protest in a summer of Vietnam War protests. The crowd, your basic good citizens with a cause, is keeping the noise down to just short of controlled shouting. It's the usual rant you've heard before...that we have no right being in Vietnam, that we're invaders in a foreign country, that our government and military are nothing but a bunch of criminals...and on and on.

Facing them down and shouting even louder are those who believe it's our sacred duty as proud Americans and caretakers of peace and freedom to protect the world from communism.

Are they kidding? The reason we're in Vietnam is because we got into this goddamn mess in the first place and we don't have a clue on how to get out of it. Years of fighting and endless casualties have rendered the U.S. powerless against the unyielding Viet Cong rebels .

Meanwhile, I couldn't care less about Vietnam. It doesn't impinge on my life one way or the other. I have a war of my own that takes precedence over this one. I just want to get through this damn crowd and over to the other side of the Common. I'm already late for my appointment.

But the debate between the two protest factions has somehow escalated to a fever pitch which, in turn, has developed into a fairly major brawl which, in turn, has erupted into a crazed mob scene with violent pushing, shouting and screaming.

And then, with all of that going on, there's a sudden lineup of cops making even more racket than the protesters, barking out orders for everyone to disperse.

What happens next tells me I many never get where I want to go. A barrage of rocks comes flying out from the crowd, one of them hitting the skull of an officer. Blood instantly appears on his forehead, just before he sinks to all fours.

"Jesus, Mary and Joseph," someone near me says, a priest with a peace placard. Implicit in his tone is that there will be trouble. The cops have been provoked, never a good sign.

The feeling in the air is that this could lead to a scene rem-iniscent of the police clashes in Selma, Alabama, back in '64, and more recently, at the Democratic National Convention in Chicago, resulting in hundreds of injuries.

Cops on horseback appear ready to charge anyone in their paths, including a contingent of moms whose sons are, at this very moment, fighting, and maybe dying, in Vietnam.

If the protesters thought they had something called freedom of speech accorded to them as a God-given right, they are sadly mistaken.

The cops, being heckled, are now ordering protesters to lie face down on the ground with their hands behind their heads. The response is a steady chanting of pig, pig, pig.

Now we're in big trouble. One cop on horseback barely misses my cranium with his truncheon and hey, I'm not even a pro-tester. I'm just a pedestrian trying to get to an appointment.

Within a few minutes, I'm witness to people being "subdued" and carried bodily to waiting paddy wagons, their heads cre-at-ing a bump, bump, bump cadence on the pavement.

One young woman is being dragged along by her ponytail. She appears acquiescent, as if just going along for the ride. T his is passive resistance to the extreme. Even Gandhi would have grabbed the cop by the throat.

I shouldn't laugh, but despite the violence, some of the stuff going on strikes me as funny—like the way the kid with the un-flattering likeness of Richard Nixon painted on his torso re-fus-es to stand up. Every time the cops get him up on his feet, he allows his upper body to fold down from the waist and his legs to buckle.

Nearby, someone sings an unintelligible, drug-induced version of "We Shall Overcome" until he, too, is dragged off by the cops.

What's next, I wonder, tear gas? With folks running every which way to avoid having their mucus membranes being set afire? The way things are turning out, it wouldn't surprise me. And yet there I go, walking smack into the middle of the melee, heedless of the danger. Anyone seeing me strolling so casually would think I was suicidal or just plain crazy. Actually, I think I must be both because, considering the mess I got myself into this morning, I don't rightly care if I am a casualty. In fact, I would welcome it.

But no such luck. I manage to move across the expanse of grass without a scratch while people on either side of me are being whacked senseless by that small, but omnipresent, bunch of cops who take pleasure in resorting to physical violence.

Nasty as all this is, I've got my own problems to deal with. Who has time for Vietnam?

- 2 -

I never refer to Bertram Perlberg as anything but Bertram, a name he detests and has repeatedly asked me not to address him by. Dr. B. Pickering Perlberg is his official name. For a shrink, he's very sensitive, always taking things personally.

I had phoned his office right after the incident this morning and was told by that he was with another patient. I told her of my intention to jump in front of an MTA trolley—not an empty threat, considering how desperate I was feeling.

Bertram's nonchalant reply, when he did deign to come to the phone, was that since I was going to kill myself, did I want to cancel my appointment? Typical Bertram sarcasm, his way of dealing with a would-be suicide.

I'm late arriving due to the riot. Bertram, instead of being some sort of comfort in my now reduced minutes with him, is instead throwing in my face everything I confided in him on the phone. He tells me what a senseless and incredibly stupid thing I did this morning when meeting with a client, as if I don't already know.

The scene of the meeting springs to mind. A team of co-workers and I are presenting an advertising campaign to one of our agency's most important clients, a pampered prince of commerce worth millions in billings who doesn't acknowledge my existence. He even takes several phone calls while I'm presenting.

We've all worked day and night getting this campaign together. My art director, also present, is too scared of the client to say anything, but his excellent visuals speak for themselves. The accompanying copy is smart and informative, proclaiming the virtues of the product, a chain of ultra-chic health spas that only the ultra-wealthy can afford.

All six ads in the campaign share the same headline: *For People Who Can't Stand Self-Indulgence in Others, But Often Forgive it in Themselves.* The self-indulgent people in the ads are beautiful, upscale women in bikinis and men very few guys are lucky enough to look like.

To get a better view of the ads, I've spread then out on the carpet near the easy-chair where the client is sitting, and to show us what he thinks of the campaign, the son of a bitch gets up and walks all over them, literally.

I'm prepared to let this go, angry as it's making me, but then he makes a motion as if he is scraping dog shit off his shoes.

This is more than I can stand. I stroll over to the client's portrait, take it off the wall, and put my foot through it.

"You abuse my property," I announce, "and I abuse yours."

This is not my line. I have borrowed it from the legendary adman, Carl Ally who, in responding to a client insulting his ads, is said to have got up from his chair, walked over to the client's rare potted fern, unzipped his fly, and proceeded to urinate on it.

If Ally's actions added to his legend, mine have caused an almighty uproar. Almost instantly the enraged client has fired the agency, an act that has resulted in the terminations of fourteen people, myself included.

"What are you planning to do now that you screwed everything up?" Good old Bertram, not mincing words. "You'll obviously have to get another job."

"Fat chance my getting another job in Boston," I say. "The news of how I single-handedly lost the account is probably all over town by now. Who'd be dumb enough to hire me? I wouldn't even hire me."

"Now why would you say such a thing?" Bertram asks, his voice and manner suddenly changed. I think *uh oh…he's doing it again.*

"You've made beautiful progress. You are smart, responsible and successful. I admire your strength and courage. With your spotless record, you are now ready to go out into the world and conquer it. You can do anything you set your mind to. Here's to your great and glorious future!"

"You don't understand, Bertram," knowing that his dementia has kicked in again, and that he has mixed me up with another patient. "I've just been fired from my job! I've got a lot of people fired! Innocent people, good people, with families. And there's my family. There's my wife, Allie, and there are my kids. I can't believe what I've done to everybody. My guilt is enormous."

But Bertram is unhearing. A voice belonging to his receptionist comes over the intercom informing him that our session is running over and that the next patient is waiting. I watch Bertram rise from his chair, walk across the room where he lets out a rather loud MEOW.

Leaving through one door while the patient I've held up enters via another, I wonder when Bertram will revert back to being human.

His receptionist rarely looks directly at a patient, but if she does, she treats him or her as if strictly normal.

"Same time next week?" she asks.

- 3 -

So much has changed in my life since Robert Kennedy was assassinated a little over a year ago. I had been with Papert, Koenig, Lois, the New York ad agency handling Kennedy's presidential campaign. We were all eating and sleeping and living our mission to get Kennedy into the White House. Then came the assassination and the account was defunct.

At that point, there was no further need for those of us who'd worked on it. What had been the most exhilarating experience in our lives was now a cold, empty void.

Kennedy's goal was to end the war in Vietnam. We'll never know how many lives, both military and civilian, would have been saved had Kennedy been able to achieve that. So Sirhan Sirhan didn't just kill one person, but maybe thousands of others.

He also killed my one chance of continuing in a top New York agency where I was able to do good work. After that, it was a series of dead ends. And then a job turned up at Pikeman and Partners in Boston which for me meant exile. I took it anyway because it was a new start in a new city where Allie would feel more secure and maybe give up drinking. Not that she ever admitted to a drinking problem. I attributed it to my job problems and my inability to tolerate imbecilic clients.

Of course all agencies have imbecilic clients like the CEO of a Fortune 500 Company who always insisted on taking the key word out of a headline, thereby rendering it inane, or the client who had to have the product name mentioned in every other sentence, as if the consumer was going to suffer total memory loss in between. But I was able to deal with the difficult clients at the Boston agency.

Until this morning.

Leaving Bertram's office and walking back across the common, the carnage is over. There are a few protestors wander around in a daze, but otherwise, all is calm.

I dread going home because I'll have to tell Allie that I am, once again, unemployed. Suddenly, I'm aware of a decision my brain has automatically made without actually consulting me—which is *not* to go home. Not right away. It's after five, so I walk to my car on Boylston Street and from there to Manny's Bar where the agency crowd hangs out after work.

- 4 -

There's a hush as I enter and I can feel all eyes on me. It's so uncomfortable, I immediately feel like walking out, but something impels me to stay. Sitting at the bar wondering what they're going to do next to get jobs are at least five "friends" who were fired from the agency because we/I lost the account.

If I'm worried about my future, they must be catatonic. No matter what else my reputation may be at the moment, I'm at least thought to have talent. They're thought to have little or none. If they ever had any, they've let advertising suck it out of them. And now, not only has the agency lost its biggest account, management has done some extra housecleaning. They've let go people from all departments—deadwood they've been labeled-- and it's all been done under the umbrella pretext that I'm to blame.

No one speaks to me. The silence is deafening. "A beer," I say to the bartender. Even he looks as if he's thinking twice about serving me. When the beer arrives, I pour it down my throat in a few gulps and then order another. I order drinks all around. That makes Stevie Dorfman, an art director, speak up.

"None for me," Stevie tells the bartender. The big, fun-loving jokester, an irreverent, mischievous, man, would have fallen all over the place laughing about damaging the client's portrait—if it hadn't cost him his job.

"None for me, either," says another, Sally Crown. She'd been with the agency her entire working life, twenty-four years. It was my action this morning that caused her to be terminated with six weeks severance and four weeks vacation pay. One more year and she would have had a pension.

"Tim!" she calls, greatly distressed by my presence. A man, a head shorter than me, comes rushing over and stands between Sally and me. He, too, has been canned.

"It's all right," I say, putting some money down on the bar. "I was just leaving," but it's too late. The little man, my friend, Tim Salway is trying to punch me. I hold him off but one of his blows makes contact, and the runt has given me a bloody nose. Then he connects with my right eye and I know it's going to be a shiner. I wonder to myself what on earth was I thinking, coming into this bar to be among the people whose lives I've ruined?

I disentangle myself from Tim, and manage to get out of the place, checking my ribs and kidneys as several Boston matrons walking by condemning me with their eyes. Other passers-by look away as people do when they don't want to get involved.

- 5 -

To get to my car in my bloodied condition, I have to put on blinders and make my way through rush-hour sidewalk traffic. Even without looking at anyone, I sense I'm a spectacle, blood running out of my nose and down my shirt.

A man asks if I'm okay and I growl: "Do I look like I'm okay?" After what seems an eternity, I reach the car and get inside fast. If it had shades, I would pull them down.

Passing the Arlington Street Church where many protesters from the doomed rally are now congregating, I see most of them are flower children, sweet and peaceful, receiving first aid. There are many injured among them, sitting dazed on the steps.

This church supports the anti-war movement and gives shelter to anyone in contention with the government. Right now, it's serving as a first aid station as well as a spiritual center.

I should stop the car and get treated myself, but I got my injuries because of an irresponsible act, not a patriotic one, so I just keep going.

Cars on Boylston are hardly moving. As I inch my way along, people in other cars look curiously at my battered face. Then they look at the car, searching it for any damage a collision might have caused. I certainly give the impression of having been in an accident.

I get curious too, and have a look in the rearview mirror. My first inclination is to shrink back from it, but it's kind of fascinating seeing your face blown up and bruised. One eye is beginning to close and I have a fat lip.

Examining my teeth, I notice that one is chipped. I practically ram the car in front of me when I see that. The chipped tooth won't make a big difference, probably won't be noticeable, but it's permanent evidence of what occurred today.

Outside the car, and somewhere outside myself, there are loud, angry horns of cars behind me. I'm suddenly aware the blaring is directed at me, personally, since I'm standing absolutely still, studying my mug in the mirror. I start up again and creep along.

Four miles and forty minutes later, I'm in Brookline, driving past the part where every other Victorian is a dilapidated rooming house for Harvard and M.I.T. students. Then past the part of town that's comfortable but not fashionable, until I reach Brookline Village, with the bigger homes with well-tended gardens and interested people doing interesting things with their lives, or so said the real estate lady who showed us the big Victorian a year ago.

Pulling into the driveway of our house on Cypress Street, I'm careful not to slam the car door, in case Allie is within earshot. I prefer to sneak in and clean up as much as possible before she sees me. Better still, if I can just keep out of sight until Allie has had the six or seven drinks she's going to down tonight, chances are she won't even notice my face.

Just as I'm about to turn the key in the front door, a tiny figure comes streaking past from the side of the house and runs bare-assed down the walk. A larger figure comes running after him with a diaper flapping in her hand.

"Charlie," Allie calls. She scoops up the child just as he's about to run into the road and gives him a smack on the bottom that outrages him. Red-faced and screaming, he tries to retaliate by urinating on her, but she swiftly sidesteps just in time, gives him another smack, and tucks him under her arm. Heading back to the garden, she spots me on the veranda.

"Oh, you're home," she says, and the expression on her face turns to something indefinable as I walk toward her.

"What's happened to your face?" Is it horror in her voice? Or happiness?

"I've been in a little accident," I say, not really caring if Allie believes me.

"A little accident?" Allie asks. "You look like what's left of a big one." We're interrupted by Angela, our five-year-old, who comes rushing toward me.

"Daddy, Daddy," she yells as I pick her up. Then, seeing my face, she recoils in horror. This is not her Daddy, but some monstrous looking person. I try to calm her without luck. She screams hysterically, fighting to be put down so she can run to her mother.

Allie soothes Angela and walks with me to the garden where I see Denise Lawson sitting perfectly still on a chaise lounge. She's a fairly new friend of Allie's and, seeing her, wish I had ducked into the house unseen. Patently cool, she observes me with the kind of interest a person might take in some new as-yet unnamed, viral strain. I'm a little surprised to see her sitting in my garden at all.

Denise is from a totally different social stratum in Boston, known as "old money." She and Allie have somehow bridged the gap. They became friends while taking a one-day quilting course together a few months before. I've never known her to come to the house.

It's Allie who is asking all the questions about the "accident", but Denise puts a casual hand through her dark hair and merely looks as if she couldn't care less.

"How's Tod?" I ask her. Tod is her husband.

"Fine," she answers coolly. I have a sudden panicky feeling that Denise may have heard, through her husband, Tod, of the catastrophe I've landed the agency in and has come to the house to inform Allie. Or, at least to be with her when she finds out.

Tod Lawson, even though he doesn't have to work, is also in advertising, more as a hobby than a vocation. He even donates his salary to Save the Children, and has political aspirations with the Republican Party.

If Tod is like everyone else in the Boston ad community, he'll be talking about the account leaving my former agency, because for one thing, it's now up for grabs among the other agencies, his included.

It's obvious that Denise hasn't said anything to Allie who is very calm, calmness being the effect having friends around has on her.

"Come into the house and I'll put something on those cuts," Allie says. Looking at Denise, I almost wish she *would* tell Allie for me. She is at her Brahmin coolest right now, regarding me without interest. I enjoy looking at her Newport-tanned legs, and can almost visualize the dark, moist place between them.

"See you," I say, as I am led into the house.

I am now face to face with Allie, one of the major problems in my life. How the hell am I going to tell her what's happened? She's stone sober.

"What kind of accident was it, Bobby?" she asks, lightly pressing a cold towel to the myriad swollen places on my face.

"Tim Salway beat me up," I reply.

"Tim?" Allie asks. I wait for her look of incredulity to disappear. I know what she is thinking. Tim is one of the mildest characters on earth.

"Well, I'd hate to see the condition he's in," she offers. "You didn't hurt him much, did you?"

"Didn't touch him."

"Bobby, what's this all about?" Allie asks in her serious voice.

"Tim was fired today," I say. "He was bitter."

"But why take it out on you? You're his friend."

"It was because of me that he was fired."

Allie is intrigued, but getting a bit apprehensive. "What do you mean?"

"There was a bloodbath at the agency—Tim, Sally, Hans..."

"Hans?"

"That's right. Good old Hans. My great, old buddy. Even he turned on me in the end."

Allie is being extremely cautious now. "You said something about you being the cause."

"That's right, I…"

"Of what?" There's a tentative quality to Allie's question.

"It's because of me that an account left the agency, and therefore it's because of me that a lot of people were fired."

"If you're going to tell me that you were fired along with them, I don't want to hear about it. Do you understand? I don't want to know. You'll just have to keep it to yourself."

Allie is suddenly trembling. This has happened so many times during our marriage, but she never gets used to it.

I'm about to speak, but before I can, Allie has headed for the back door to the security of her friend. She has ceased bothering about my injuries. As she goes out, she looks back at me with bitterness written on her face, green eyes caught in a shaft of sunshine.

"If you've got yourself canned, just keep it to yourself. Leave the house the same time tomorrow morning that you usually do, and come home tomorrow the same time you usually do. I don't care what you do in between."

"Thanks," I say sarcastically, in time with the screen door banging shut. Upstairs, I strip to take a shower. In the bedroom mirror, I survey the damage done by Tim's flailing fists. Looks worse than it is, but one eye is plastered shut.

I begin to imagine I shall lose the eye, which plunges me into a self-pity session. I'm thinking about my lost life, and gazing down the full-length mirror, I think about my lifeless member. Picking it up in my hand, I look down at it, dead and grayish. The door to the bedroom opens and it's Denise Lawson. I stand there holding it in my hand.

"One of the kids is in the downstairs bathroom and Allie said there was a guest john up here," she says, looking at me standing there, holding it.

"That's right," I say, as if giving somebody traffic directions. "It's right down the hall. First door on the left."

"Thanks," she says, closing the door behind her.

-6-

Later, much later, in the middle of the night, I whisper "Allie" and get no response though I know she's awake.

Like me, she can't sleep due to worry. I went to bed at seven, without having reappeared downstairs or having said goodnight to the children. If I hadn't gone to bed so early, I wouldn't be wide-awake now at 4a.m., waiting for some sign that there's going to be another day—not that I want another day, especially if it's going to be the kind of day yesterday was.

Lying here, I get the feeling that morning has been postponed indefinitely. The hands on the illuminated clock refuse to move. Getting out of bed at this hour is out of the question. What would I do with myself?

Sleep eventually returns. Out of habit, I slip my arm around Allie's shoulders. When times were better than they are now, we would remain in this same position until my arm would nearly fall off from a lack of circulation.

I'm sure that if I told Allie I loved her, she would say that she loved me, too, but during this critical moment when I'm helping myself to a giant portion of self-contempt, that's the one thing I certainly don't want to hear.

When morning does come, I see that Allie must be dreaming something pretty terrific because she smiles and stretches and turns over on her tummy, bending her wrist under her throat the way she does when she cuddles up to herself. It's only when she opens her eyes and sees me looking straight into them that the look of happiness is wiped off her face.

"What time is it?" she asks in monotone.

"What does it matter?" I answer.

Nothing from her for a moment, then: "It doesn't." She wearily gets out of bed to face another day.

-7-

In all my years in the advertising business, I have worked at many locations in Manhattan, though only once on Madison Avenue. But wherever I've worked—whether on Lexington Avenue or Third Avenue or Park Avenue South—they were all considered Madison Avenue.

Madison Avenue is anywhere and everywhere advertising takes place. It's Buffalo and Minneapolis and Tuscaloosa. It even stretches across the oceans to London, Paris, Tokyo, Casablanca; they are all Madison Avenue.

My first Madison Avenue job was far from that fabled thoroughfare, all the way west on 34th Street in Manhattan. It was at the old J.C. Penney Building near Tenth Avenue, or almost as far as you can get west without falling into the Hudson River.

I arrived there for an interview as a junior copywriter one freezing November day, lured by an ad in the *New York Daily News* for copywriter trainees at the grand salary of $80 a week. At a time when yearly wages of $2,500 a year were average, $80 a week was a fortune.

Looking back in my memory's eye, I see the man who interviewed me, the copy chief, Chet Kellogg. I must have looked strange the way I was dressed, in my brother's metallic blue raincoat, buttoned to the neck, but he didn't say anything about it.

The fact was, I had no interview clothes. I borrowed my brother's raincoat because the clothes I did have were frayed and moth-eaten. They had been worn daily for the past few months and had simply given out. My shirt had been washed so regularly that it was practically transparent. Completing the ensemble were the Charlie Chaplin baggy pants and the jacket with the baggy elbows.

At the time of this interview, I was a gofer at CBS, the lowest person on the totem pole. Even the ushers snubbed me. And I was always making my boss mad, like the time I was ordered to walk a famous female star's dog in snowy Central Park, and it got loose. I spent a frantic hour searching for a white poodle in a white landscape. Had I not found the dog I probably would not have returned to work, but I finally caught up with her.

"Where did you take the damn dog, Toronto?" my boss yelled when I finally got back.

"She wouldn't pee," I replied, and kept my job.

So now I had a new job at J.C. Penney. Chet hired me and assigned me to the J.C. Penny Catalog. But first I underwent a copy training course with a group of other cubs.

That's when a young woman appeared at my desk to tell me something. She was Allie Scott, a copy supervisor, extremely good-looking, extremely haute-couture, and extremely apprehensive, probably because by then I had a reputation as a weirdo. Just before Christmas, it was announced that a list of employee addresses would be handed out so that people could send cards to one another.

To me, printing someone's name on a list without getting prior permission was an invasion of privacy. So, going to the personnel department to complain, I found that it was too late to revise the lists, but not too late for me to cut my name and address out of each with scissors. This caused a ripple through the agency with people talking about me in the same way they might talk about Jack the Ripper. In fact, I was given the name Bob the Snipper.

So no wonder Allie looked so nervous approaching me. "You are going to work with me," she hesitantly announced. It was apparent to me that she was dubious about this arrangement. I was, no doubt, foisted upon her by Chet Kellogg and who knows, perhaps she had pleaded to have him assign me to somebody else, *anybody* else.

"You'll be glad to know," she continued, "that you and I have our own office. Most of the writers are situated in cubicles, so this is a plus. Your contribution to the catalog will be in writing men's and women's shoe copy. Apparently, management feels you have had ample time to learn the preferred J.C. Penney writing style and that you've met the required criteria."

"Why are you talking that way?" I asked.

"What way?" she asked, totally taken aback.

"Like a corporate robot."

"I am doing no such thing," she declared. Suddenly, her lovely peaches and cream complexion was starting to look a little like borsht.

"When do we start?" I asked, aware that I had the upper hand in this, our first exchange.

"Look, if you don't want this assignment, why don't you talk to Chet about it," Allie said. "I'm sure he could place you somewhere else."

"Who said I didn't want this assignment?"

"Okay then. Be in room 518 at nine sharp tomorrow, and may I request that you leave your nastiness behind?"

"Sorry, but my nastiness goes wherever I go." I was going to tease her some more, but she had already walked off.

- 8 -

I'm back in Bertram's office even though it's Wednesday, not Friday. I can't wait till Friday. I'm desperate, even if it means talking to someone who thinks he is a cat.

In the reception area, I spot the latest Life Magazine. If the bloody Boston Common protest didn't get to me, this issue reporting the carnage in Vietnam, along with the photos of all those young American lives cut short, certainly does. In the last few years, there have been nine major battles in Vietnam, including the Tet offensive and the battle for Hue.

It doesn't look like this thing is going to end any time soon. Former President Lyndon Johnson, taking the advice given him by Secretary of Defense Robert McNamara and National Security Advisor, Henry Kissinger, ordered the escalation of troops to "Veetnam," as he pronounced it, from 50,000 in 1963 to 500,000 in 1965. "Mah fellow 'Merkins," Johnson would say, likely unaware that a merkin is a (false) pubic hair-piece, "we are going to win this thing...."

With media coverage revealing images of civilians, notably woman and children killed by our use of napalm, and the mounting toll of Americans brought home in body bags, "Hey, hey, LBJ, how many kids have you killed today?" became a protest chant. Now we have Richard Nixon as president. I'm thinking about that when Bertram's secretary tells me he's finally able to see me.

First thing I do is plead. "Bertram, for God's sake, if you can't do anything for me, do something for Allie."

"Allie is not my patient. You are my patient," he says. "All I can do is advise you."

"Then advise me, Bertram. Advise me instead of just sitting there looking pretty."

"You're wasting your hostility on me," Bertram says. "I've told you time and again that I don't take anything a patient says personally. So let's just drop all this bullshit and get on with the session."

Now that Bertram has lost his rag a little, I feel in control of the situation again. "Right on, Doc."

"Tell me what you've been doing since last session," he says, deliberately calmer.

"Nothing. I've been doing nothing."

"No job interviews?"

"No job interviews."

"Why not?"

"Nobody will see me. I've been calling the agencies and the message I get is that there are no openings and there never will be an opening for me. I can't even get through to Lorne Chambers."

"Lorne Chambers?"

"I've told you about Lorne at least ten times, Bertram. He's the one I used to identify with as a brother."

"Ah yes, I remember," Bertram says, looking blank.

"He was supposed to have been my best friend. His secretary told me he would call back. He never has."

"It could be that he's extremely busy," Bertram rationalizes. "Or perhaps he doesn't have a job to offer you and doesn't know how to tell you. After all, he's only human."

"Listen Bertram, when I came up here to Boston, he followed right after me, couldn't bear to be away from me. That's because without me, he didn't know how to do an ad. I wrote most of the stuff he is known for. And where did my work get him? A job as creative director of a big Boston ad agency."

"You may have helped him, but he must be quite capable in his own right to have achieved so much success."

"Bertram, why do you think I come here? I have serious problems. I'm on the street with no prospects and Lorne hasn't called me once. He must have found someone else to do his dirty work."

Bertram is relentless with his tiresome, devil's advocate approach. "Could it be you've turned against Lorne because you're angry with yourself?"

"Is it time?" I ask in reply.

"Time for what?"

"Time for me to get outta here," I say. "I don't want to waste my time and money if you are going in that direction. Lorne is a slimy son of a bitch and that's all there is to it. And, by the way, I just caught you sneaking a look at that little clock you have hidden across the room in all those plants."

"You still have three minutes," Bertram answers composedly. "But tell me, what about the headhunters? Don't they have any job interviews to send you on?"

"Yeah," I answer, "if I want to move to Lagos or Rangoon."

"Are you thinking of leaving Boston?"

I know what Bertram is thinking: the money I owe him.

"No," I say, "my shrink is here." I catch him looking at his goddamned clock again. I ask him to give me some kind of advice about Allie before I leave."

"Who's Allie?" he asks.

- 9 -

The feeling I have these days is that I'm leaning on thin air, lacking any kind of support. I'm out there on my own and it's scary. I know people in the ad community are talking about me, and I've heard the outrageous story going around that it wasn't the client's portrait I put my foot through, but a *Chagall*.

It's amazing how facts get distorted. If it had been a Chagall, I would be facing a stiff prison sentence and I would be paying restitution for the rest of my life.

As it is, I can hardly pay the bills. Our savings are rapidly running out. Frozen peas are up to thirty-nine cents. Milk is now eighteen cents a half gallon. Gas is up to thirty cents a gallon.

Having no job or the prospect of one, I try to be useful doing things around the house for Allie, and going on errands, such as to the supermarket. Going directly to the market from Bertram's, I push the grocery wagon around to the canned cha-cha version of "Cheek to Cheek."

Up ahead, a housewife in hair-curlers sways her hips as she cha-chas from detergents to the canned vegetables. Her lips are moving to "Heaven, I'm in heaven…." Throwing caution to the winds, her wagon is bulging. Probably she came to the store for a half-dozen eggs and the rhythm got to her. Even the most price-sensitive customers can fall victim to canned music. To entice people like this is one of the things I hate most about being in the ad biz.

Coming up to the checkout counter, I find myself behind Denise Lawson. She no doubt has various people on her household staff to shop, but the enormously wealthy Denise likes to give the impression of someone down-to-earth enough to do certain plebian tasks, such as grocery-shopping. It's only when she begins to unload her wagon that she notices me.

"Why, hello." Her smile is rather warm. For her.

"Why, hello back," I reply. For some reason I don't feel at all embarrassed about the bathroom episode. At least not as embarrassed as I felt right after it happened.

"And how is Allie?" she asks brightly, knowing perfectly well that Allie is miserable. She's been commiserating with her on a daily basis. That doesn't annoy me. Allie needs someone to commiserate with. I do feel, however, that she's been campaigning for Allie to leave me. How do I know that? I don't. I just feel it.

"Allie's fine, " I reply, mimicking her brightness. "How's Tod?"

"Just fine." Sudden end of conversation. The checkout girl has totaled the bill while another girl has packed Denise's groceries for her. While the checker is processing my stuff, I say good-bye to Denise Lawson and watch her walk out of the store, twitching her neat little butt.

It isn't five minutes later that I demolish the right rear fender of her Lincoln Continental convertible while coming around a blind spot on the side of the store.

-10-

As we get out of our cars, Denise is less cordial than she was in the store. "Maybe you were admiring yourself in the mirror again," she says pointedly. "And maybe you should have had *both* hands on the steering wheel…"

"You never play with yourself," I want to say. But instead: "You might want to get your driver's license ready. Here comes the fuzz." A lone, unsmiling policeman gets slowly out of his patrol car and approaches us. He silently surveys the damage.

"Who was driving the car in back?" he asks.

"Looks like I was," I say with a feeble little laugh.

"Well, you came around the bend too fast, it looks like," the policeman says.

"Correction. I came around the corner at the normal speed. The lady stopped short."

Denise smiles at the policeman. "Officer, tell Mr. Bronson the law, will you please? How the driver in the rear is always responsible for rear collisions."

"How did I know you were going to come to a complete halt on a blind curve?" I say, but I know Denise and her smile and the obvious fact that she's wealthy have already won over the cop.

"Perhaps you need a refresher course in how to drive," Denise says.

"Well," says the cop, "there's no need to argue. Your insurance will take care of it."

"That's right," I say. "Denise, what are we arguing about? It was a simple accident. Our insurance will cover it. Why don't we park these two wrecks someplace and have a drink?"

"I think," says Denise with a mischievous twinkle in her eye, "you've had enough to drink."

The policeman, suddenly very red-faced, is breathing down my neck. "Hey, have you been drinking?"

"Well, maybe one or two at lunch…"

"You'll have to come with me," the policeman says. "Park your car over there, roll up the windows and lock the doors.

"Now, just a min__"

Down at the station, I blow into a balloon attached to a gauge that shows the amount of alcohol in my bloodstream. Then I wait for the report.

"You can go, Mr. Bronson," the policeman says after two hours. "You don't show much alcohol.

Ten minutes later, I pull up in Denise Lawson's driveway.

-11-

The smashed-up Continental is abandoned near the stables, the passenger door left open. Probably she'll just discard this car, rather than have it repaired.

The grounds surrounding the house are smartly manicured; a virtual mini-Versailles. Several landscape gardeners work in the distance. I've never been in the Lawson house before, but I've heard a lot about it. It's one of the biggest houses in Brookline, and said to be one of the most beautiful.

Climbing the steps to the front door, I'm feeling damned angry. Denise is supposed to be a friend of Allie's. She could have gotten me into a lot of trouble. I press hard and long on the doorbell.

"What kept you so long?" Denise says, opening the door almost immediately.

"What the hell are you talking about?"

"I knew you'd come. I was certain of it. Come in. Toddy won't be home for hours."

A thousand thoughts suddenly crash into one another in my brain as I follow Denise into her exquisite, *Architectural Digest*-worthy living room.

"Have a drink," Denise says. The look on her face implies only one thing. I look at her for a long moment and finally turn away.

"You gotta be kidding."

Outside in the car are all the groceries that Allie's waiting for. My greatest fear is the butter must be melting.

Denise pours me a double scotch. There's a slight smile on her face.

"Well," I say, taking the drink and looking into Denise's determined eyes. I notice that one eye is slightly smaller than the other. "Here's to you."

Denise ignores my toast. She's obviously ready for the bedroom. Or maybe she wants to do it in the sitting room. I notice there are no household servants around. Either she told them she didn't wish to be disturbed, or sent them home. After all, she was certain I would come, and had plenty of time to get rid of them.

When I do nothing, she sits back. From her facial expression, she is conveying that I'm not man enough to take her up on her unspoken, but oh so clear, proposition.

"You have the wrong guy," I say. "I'm married to one of your best friends, remember? Why don't you get one of the gardeners?"

Denise doesn't reply, but stands up and with one swift movement, lets her dress fall to the floor. She's a woman, all right. Two breasts, pussy, the works. And she's brown all over, a luxury of the super-rich.

Right then and there I decide I'm not going to have intercourse with her, but will simply pleasure her. I gently lower her to the couch. I move down to her legs and rest my head between them.

Denise lets out little cries as I circle the area between her legs with my tongue. She shudders, arching her back, and yells something unintelligible, although it sounds like "Daddy." I make fast, rhythmic movements until, quite abruptly, my jaw and neck become rigid with a cramp.

"What is it?" Denise asks, startled. "What's the matter?" She tries to push my head back into place. I get up and walk quickly around the room in agonizing pain. My jaw and neck refuse to relax. I hold my neck with both hands in a way that suggests I'm strangling myself.

Denise is watching me from the couch, propped up on one elbow, intrigued. I feel my eyes will pop out of my head at any moment.

"Can't you do something for it?" Denise asks, irritated. The cramp won't quit. To relieve it, I start jumping first on one foot and then the other. Finally, the cramp starts to recede.

Denise lies back and I resume my position until a few seconds later, a second cramp cripples me. I used to be able to keep doing it for hours, but obviously, I'm very much out of practice.

My jaw is gaping and my neck-bone protrudes painfully. Denise stands up, mumbling something about me being a eunuch. She goes out of the room disgusted as I leap around in agony.

Later, I look around and find her sitting naked in the kitchen, having a drink and a cigarette. "Facial cramps," I explain, but she says nothing.

In the car going home, I know I've disappointed Denise, but my thoughts don't dwell on that because I don't give a damn about her. They dwell on Allie. I feel terrible that I allowed myself to be drawn into a situation with Denise. The guilt is tremendous. I vow never again to let anything like this happen.

-12-

Allie...when we first met. What was I trying to prove at J.C. Penney by treating her that way? It wasn't personal. Anyone who'd had the misfortune of having me assigned to them was in for it. Probably it was the old sabotage part of me that was out to get me.

She treated me in with constraint at first--as you would with an errant child. Or someone extremely disturbed. She was making the best of a bad situation, acting in an officious way so as to get through each day, paying no heed to my childish behavior, maybe even praying I would quit or get fired.

Our office was longer than it was wide—with her desk near the front door and mine near a rear door. The buyers all had offices on the same floor, including a guy who was not our boss, but somehow thought he was; Walter Dunfrey, buyer for men's, women's and children's shoes.

Dunfrey was a hard-working, regular kind of guy in his early forties. He was very practical and brusque at times, with a no-nonsense demeanor. A husband and father of four or five kids, he wore a girdle. Okay, not a girdle, but the same kind of thing so as to support his back.

He let me know right off what he expected of me. I was to write all the copy for men's shoes to his absolute specifications and for his ultimate approval. I was to consider him my boss, and although it wasn't exactly stated, I was to cower any time he disapproved of my work.

Of course, there was no way in hell that I was going to do any of those things. So from the beginning, Walter Dunfrey and I were in contention, though it was never full-blown contention. I didn't give it much thought.

I was far more interested in the unfolding of Allie. She lived a glamorous life, wore designer clothes, had a large following of sophisticated men and women friends with whom she was smitten.

There was one, a blond man who wore a camel-hair overcoat and white silk scarf, Beau Bennett. He had a pedigree background to go with the camel hair. Each morning, he would appear at our office so Allie could knot his tie for him. Often he would return around noon and take her for a $300.00 lunch at Le Pavilion or Twenty-one.

Beau wasn't her only suitor. Allie had a bevy of rich and successful men vying for her time and attention. I would hear her laughing at their jokes and innuendos when they phoned her making dates for evening trysts and weekends in the Hamptons.

I waited a full month before I made my move. Never once dreaming that she would accept, but with money in my pocket now that I was getting regular paychecks, I asked her out for a drink. Unbelievably, she accepted.

The first part of the date is something of a blur, but the hotel isn't. I remember that Allie was packing away vermouth on the rocks, while I was drinking boilermakers to impress her and she was definitely impressed. It was after many rounds of drinks that I reached over and kissed her—and by the time that was over, I knew all her dental work.

It was only natural to suggest we spend the rest of the night together. Thinking she would never go for that, I was wrong. We chose the Plaza Hotel.

That first sex—impatient, fiery, with exquisite movement—sent us both into some far-off land where we lost our minds for the duration. I was twenty-four at the time, a year older than Allie, and so I could happily do my part in us losing our minds quite frequently that night. Allie did the rest. Expertly.

The Buddhists have a saying about the early delicious days of a relationship being "the ripening of poisonous fruit." If only I knew what lay ahead for us, I would have leapt out of that bed, thrown on my clothes, and run away as fast as I could have.

Those vermouths on the rocks were not just something to drink for Allie. They were like oxygen, and the thirst for that oxygen would increase with time until, tragically, she became a full-fledged alcoholic.

At first, it never occurred to me that she was an alcoholic. My job was to make sure she had a sufficient supply of wine and when the bottles piled up, to bag them and put them out for the garbage man.

Alcoholics, to my way of thinking in those days, drank from morning to night. Allie never drank during the day. But she made up for it every evening.

In our present situation, maybe getting sloshed saves her from having to wonder how she ever got into this relationship with me, with a man who can't hold a job. In our marriage she has been free from worry for only brief periods.

And now this thing with Denise. I'm completely overcome with guilt. How could I ever let something like that happen? For me to even consider myself being unfaithful astounds me. I've made a promise to God and myself that it will never happen again, I swear it.

Pulling into the drive and rushing into the house full of love for Allie, I find her sitting in the kitchen, the late-afternoon sun streaming through the window. She's quiet, as if meditating, as I walk up to her from behind and kiss her neck. She looks up with a vast dullness in her eyes.

"Denise just called," Allie says. "She told me everything."

-13-

The sanitation people come to collect trash every Wednesday at six in the morning. Considering what I have put Allie through, I wish they would collect me.

Maybe it's because the sanitation workers aren't allowed to sleep late in their warm, comfy beds that they purposely throw garbage cans around making one hell of a racket.

Allie lies next to me as the trucks shake, rattle and roll their way up Cypress Street. They've awakened her as well. She stares at the ceiling, unwilling to talk.

Ironically, she is not angry with Denise, and for some reason that can only be explained by female logic, seems even closer to her.

But I'm left out in the cold.

The door opens. It's our daughter, Angela. "I want my breakfast," she announces.

"You had breakfast yesterday, sweetheart," I tell her, and for a moment, she thinks I'm serious.

"Oh, Daddy," she says when she realizes I'm teasing her. I look into her lovely little face as she stands by the bed. Her wispy blonde hair and blue eyes stun the senses with their freshness. I get out of bed and put on my bathrobe. On the way downstairs, I scoop Charlie out of his crib. Stephen is still asleep.

"Do you want chocolate sauce or raspberry topping on your cornflakes?" I ask Angela.

"Chocolate," Angela answers.

"Don't tell your mother," I whisper as I spoon chocolate out of a jar and apply it in rings on her cereal. This little treat is a bit of reparation for what I consider serous war-crimes against my family.

"Daddy," Angela says, watching me adoringly, "are you going to pick me up from Mrs. O' Dell's again today?" Mrs. O'Dell is the daycare lady.

"Sure, honey." I've been picking her up a lot since being out of work.

Angela digs into her cornflakes and I try to wake myself up over a cup of black coffee. "Mrs. O' Dell says you're the only daddy who comes to get us. That the other daddies all have to work."

"Mrs. O'Dell is right," I say and try to leave it at that.

"Mrs. O ' Dell says she never seen a daddy come for a child."

"Mrs. O'Dell is right," I say again, wanting to kill Mrs. O'Dell. To change the subject, I suggest we sing a few songs. "Old McDonald had a Farm" is the first choice.

"Stop songing," Stephen says from the doorway, rubbing the sleep out of his eyes. I grab him up and swing him into a chair. He's irritable because he knows Angela, Charlie and I have spent a few minutes without him and he's jealous.

"Hey," I say enthusiastically, "how would you kids like to go to the beach today instead of going to daycare?" Considering I've neglected to do anything with them this summer, taking them to the beach at Plum Island in New Hampshire seems like a good idea.

"What's a beach?" Stephen asks.

"It's the Adlanddick Ocean," Angela answers for me. "You swim there like you swim in a swimming pool."

"Can I swim in the shallow end?"

"Sure," I tell him just as Allie comes into the kitchen. She's not looking too good.

"Can he swim in the shallow end of what?" Allie asks, pouring herself a cup of coffee.

"He wants to know if he can swim in the shallow end of the Atlantic Ocean. I thought I would take them to the beach today."

Allie drinks her coffee silently, too silently. I know what's bugging her. Aside from what happened with Denise, she thinks I ought to be out looking for work. I would be, too, except I don't know where else to look.

I'm washed-up in Boston. There's even an article in the local advertising muckraker describing the incident, and how I lost a five million-dollar account for the agency, which caused the firing of agency personnel, including me.

I still keep hoping Lorne Chambers will phone me. But Lorne has never been one to stick his neck out. I've even called him at home, getting his wife, Dina, who nervously said he was away on business, shooting commercials in Norway. Knowing all of Lorne's clients, I can't imagine which one would send a film crew to Norway.

"Listen, Allie," I say, "Would you like to go to beach with us?"

"I've got housework," Allie says. "And you've got things to do yourself, haven't you?" Allie has never been one to discuss our problems which have been so many, in front of the children. But now she has started to cry. Angela and Stephen with their mouths ringed in chocolate, are unnaturally silent...

"Allie__" I start to say...

"Don't speak," Allie says. "Just don't speak."

"I was just going to say I'll take my work around the agencies today. I don't have any appointments, but maybe somebody will see me."

"I want to go to the beach," Angela says.

"Me too," says Stephen.

"Well, you can't," Allie cries. "He's got to find a job." The tears are rolling down Allie's face and the kids aren't eating.

"Your mother is right, kids. I'd better get the job thing out of the way, and then we can go to the beach. Tell you what, though, I'll take you to the beach on Saturday. How does that grab you?"

Angela starts crying first, then Stephen. As I leave the kitchen, all three of them are in tears. Then Charlie starts howling. The kids are looking at me with their accusing little eyes, and Allie has turned away.

-14-

In the midst of the current mess I've created, I think about what Allie's life would be if she'd married Beau Bennett, or else one of those other rich guys escorting her around town, lusting after her, calling her night and day. For all those mornings that Beau had arrived on his tie-tying mission, he had never looked at or regarded me as anyone of consequence. But that was soon to change.

The morning after Allie and I had gone to bed together, there was Beau entering our office, waiting for Allie to do her special job. He walked in, all Aquascutum and Abercrombie & Fitch, Princeton University, old money, Jaguar parked in a garage up the street.

I got up from my desk and stood behind Allie, cupping both her breasts in my palms. For a moment I thought Beau was going to be struck dumb. He just stared, uncomprehendingly. Allie, meanwhile, merely smiled, looking him straight in the eye.

That smile said it all. It said she was happy my hands were cupping her breasts and without a doubt, she and I were now engaged in a carnal relationship that took her right off the market as a potential girlfriend or wife. Red-faced and stunned, Beau stuttered something unintelligible and finally, awkwardly, almost tripping, turned and stumbled out of the office, never to be seen again.

But he had, before leaving, finally looked at me a long, bitter moment and unmistakably, regarded me as someone, if not of consequence, who'd bettered him for all he was worth.

Poor old Beau Bennett. I wonder whatever became of him.

-15-

Having promised Allie I would attempt to find some work, I start getting myself ready. While the shower water pours down upon me, the TV is on in the bedroom. It's the news and I can hear some of it, students rioting at some college or other and some radical, black group in California sparring with the police. And of course, Vietnam War news with the latest toll of battle-dead. More than last week, but not as many as the week before.

But then, for a change, there's something not depressing happening, something exciting. Astronauts getting ready for a landing on the moon scheduled for any day now.

Then I hear the muffled sound of the phone. A phone call is a rarity in our house these days, unless it's Beryl, Allie's sister, or Denise. Something tells me this time the phone call is for me, and a few moments later, Allie appears opaque on the other side of the shower curtain.

"Bunny Berger is on the phone," she says. There's more than a hint of expectancy in her voice, and why shouldn't there be? Bunny Berger gets jobs for people in advertising.

"Tell her I'll be right there," I say. Leaving the shower water running and grabbing a towel, I leave wet footprints all the way to the phone. I feel like I'm sweating underneath the shower water that clings to me.

Bunny Berger is one of the biggest of all headhunters in America and makes me nervous. She's to advertising what Hitler was to Germany. In truth, there's little to tell them apart, except that nobody challenges Bunny. No gathering of Allies call a D-Day on her. The creative people of advertising are like sheep, doing as she bids them. They allow her to take them out of one job and into another at an alarming rate. The fees she collects for all those "moves" have made her an extremely wealthy woman.

Fail to do as Bunny Berger demands and watch out! She has a flamethrower for a tongue and she'll use it on anyone, anytime. It's imperative not to let Bunny know how desperate you are. Fear and desperation are the two things she trades on, that she's built her empire on. I pick up the phone. "Bunny?"

"Just a moment," says a female voice, obviously the operator's. "Is this Mr. Robert Bunyon?"

"Bronson," I say.

"This is a collect call from Miss Bunny Berger in New York. Do you accept the charges, Mr. Bunyon?"

I hesitate for a moment, remembering how the Wall Street Journal recently listed Bunny Berger's earnings for the previous year at 1.3 million dollars. I consider telling the operator that I won't accept the charges, but Allie is in the room making the bed and tidying up, and listening.

"I'll accept them, yes," I say.

"Hello Bunny," I say, hoping I sound casual.

"Who is this?" a voice demands. There is no doubting that this trademark cackle belongs to Bunny Berger. It scrapes the inner ear.

"It's Bob Bronson. You called me?"

"Just a minute," she snaps. "I'm talking to someone *important*," and clicks off.

Should I hang up? Should I hold on? I want so much not to be holding this phone in my hand, but I've accepted the charges, and along with the charges, the humiliation. Allie is still in the room, supposedly dusting a table. I owe it to her to find out what this is all about—so I wait for what seems an age, cursing under my breath.

Finally, after five minutes, with me paying, Bunny returns.

"Now, Bob, what can I do for you?" She asks this in a somewhat friendlier tone. I barely keep civil.

"I was under the impression that you called me," I say tightly.

"Ah," she says, "but it was you who accepted the charges. There must have been a reason..."

The woman is both obnoxious and correct. But before I can reply, she clicks off to take another call.

Once upon a time, during a similar kind of call, I actually did hang up on Bunny Berger. She wanted to collect a fee for a job she hadn't placed me in and was trying to solicit my help in this unethical endeavor. I'd refused. And for the next year or so, the word mysteriously got around that I was really quite an extraordinary copywriter, that I had everything, except talent.

Bunny, with all the venom of a serial hit-woman, had black-listed me. People in the ad business were frightened out of their wits of getting a similar tag as the one she'd given me. Anyone thought to be associating with me might become the next Berger victim.

Because of this, I had to take jobs in lesser agencies where I would either quit or be fired. The reason was always the same—I would refuse to do inferior work and, as mentioned before, would never compromise.

Finally, after a bunch of agencies and a reputation as a hard-head, I miraculously got into the prestigious Papert, Koenig, Lois advertising agency where our biggest account was the Robert F. Kennedy presidential campaign. But after Kennedy's murder and I had moved my family to Boston, it seemed Bunny's tentacles hadn't yet reached there. I never thought I would stay in permanent exile, just until somebody down in New York had the common decency to kill her.

However, no one volunteered, and she went on to infiltrate and gobble up the entire New England area, systematically destroying the small, hometown employment agencies that were her competition.

And now she was the supreme superpower in Boston without having to take even one step out of her posh Park Avenue offices. The thought of her presence in Boston struck terror into my heart.

But what was I worrying about? Was there anything she could do to destroy my career in Boston that I hadn't already done to myself?

Still hanging onto the damn phone, I'm on the verge of hanging up, but can't make myself do it. This is the first business call I've had in weeks and because Allie is hopeful this dreadful woman will tell me about a job, I don't hang up.

Bunny clicks back on. "Bob, darling," she coos, now in her kittenish mood, "you must hate me. But don't hate me so much and I'll tell you something nice. Does the purdy little puddycat want to know what that is? They're looking for a copy chief at Abbott, Ayler, Ballard in Boston."

She waits until she knows she has me by the short hairs. Then she asks: "Interested?" Who wouldn't be interested in what could very well be a person's last chance ever?

Abbott, Ayler, Ballard is the biggest agency in Boston. It also enjoys the enviable position of being a branch office of one of the world's largest advertising conglomerates, with offices in London, Paris, Rome, Frankfurt, Tokyo, Cairo, Sydney, Caracas, Johannesburg and twenty two regional American cities, the worldwide headquarters being New York.

If AAB/Worldwide were a country, it would be the size of Brazil. To the provincial Boston advertising community, lacking the clout of such a mega-power, it therefore appears that AAB/Boston, sitting loftily on the forty-first floor of the Cunningham Building, is without a care in the world—which is true.

The prospect of becoming someone as important as the copy chief of a lush, profitable, above-it-all agency such as this is instantly tantalizing. What a comeback it would mean! Right into a top job in the Pentagon of Boston advertising agencies. I'd be back in circulation, that's for sure. Who knows, Lorne Chambers might even feel it safe enough to return my phone calls.

My mind is racing. The possibilities are endless. This is the job I want, sight unseen. I can visualize it, feel it, taste it. But I'm

LEANING ON THIN AIR

very careful not to let this vulture, Bunny Berger, know it.

"Well?" she shrieks impatiently into the phone.

"I just don't know. I guess I could be interested."

"Well, don't knock yourself out," she says nastily. "There are a dozen people up there who would give their left nut for that job."

"Then why don't you recommend them?" I say, immediately regretting I've said it, worried I have gone too far in showing "disinterest."

"*I already have,*" she says stabbingly.

"__You have?"

"They want you."

"They want me??" I'm amazed, flabbergasted.

"God only knows why, but that's it. They want you. Or to be more specific, John Quentin wants you."

"John Quentin?"

"You've heard of John Quentin, haven't you?" Again, the nasty overtone.

"Of course, I've heard of Quentin," I say. "But I didn't think he'd ever heard of me..."

"Honey, *everybody* has heard of you. You're practically a legend in your own lifetime. Quentin told me to get the guy who put a foot through the client's Chagall."

"It wasn't a Chagall." I say.

"Fine, whatever you say, but whatever it was, you're the guy he wants. God only knows why."

John Quentin is the Executive Creative Director of AAB in New York. He also oversees the creative departments of the Boston and Philadelphia branches.

I immediately do a mental review of Quentin. A dynamic force since the age of twenty-one, he is one of the best-regarded people in corporate advertising, his campaigns helping gross billions in revenues and his slogans becoming part of the American lexicon. His output has been far more conservative than mine, a lot less innovative, so I can't understand why he would be interested in me.

"What does this job pay, anyway?" I ask with a yawn in my inflection. I want to keep Bunny off the scent that I would in any way consider this the opportunity of a lifetime, *the* opportunity of my lifetime.

"Thirty five thousand, plus stock after a year, plus a car," Bunny says. "Of course, if I were you, I'd ask for more money instead of a car."

At thirty five thousand, Quentin is serious, all right. This is twice what most top executives take home.

"What do you need a car for?" Don't you already have a car?" Bunny is going on about the car, obviously because she can't charge a car on her commission. As it is, she stands to take in a twenty percent fee from the agency totaling $7,000 just for having made a few phone calls, including this one to me, which she isn't even paying for.

Come to think of it, it must be very pleasing to have a couple of dozen or so huge commissions each week. Plus the mid-sized ones like this one, and countless smaller ones.

"If I were you, I would hold out for forty and the hell with the car."

"Okay, Bunny, you win. Forty grand. No car."

"Now I didn't say I could get you forty," Bunny backtracks. "I can only try. But if I were you, I'd be in Quentin's office at 10.30 tomorrow morning. I've already made the appointment."

-16-

On the plane to LaGuardia, the pilot announces we'll be arriving ten minutes early. It's as if the gods are rushing me along to meet with yet another god, John Quentin, slogan master of "Go soak your head with Volmer's Shampoo" and other extremely successful--and in my opinion, extremely corny theme lines of the '50s and early '60s.

The first thing anyone sees when they step off the elevator at Abbott, Ayler, Ballard/New York, is an impressive list of the many AAB offices around the globe, ostentatiously lit up in neon. The light gives off a greenish cast throughout the reception area.

AAB/New York is powerful for sure, but no matter how big or powerful it is, its creative product is the direct opposite of the really extraordinary work being done at such agencies as Doyle, Dane, Bernbach and my old alma mater, Delehanty, Kurnit, and Geller.

Over the past four or five years, a different kind of advertising, never before seen and truly startling, has been done by a new generation of brash, irreverent creative people.

Having been part of that generation of brash, irreverent creatives, I've always been contemptuous of establishment agencies like AAB. I'm still contemptuous, but hardly in a position to stick my nose up. I need a job.

I'm not there very long when someone says "You the joker here to see Quentin?" I look up from my seat and see a big, greenish, hulking figure standing over me.

It's a woman who, in the strange light, is absolutely scary-looking. She's built like a Sherman tank and I'm sure she operates as one, too, with turret eye slits. I imagine those slits looking out on the world, searching out and circumventing any attempt to infiltrate her boss's domain.

I answer that yes, I am the very same joker, and am escorted to Quentin's office. What I see outside his door is a long line of people who somehow look like refugees from a war-torn country. These are copywriters and art directors waiting to see Quentin, to have him look at their work, to either approve or trash it.

They eye me as if to say: "Who the fuck is this guy cutting in front of us?" It's as if I'm some sort of visiting royalty.

The royalty I am visiting immediately gets up from his desk and greets me with the whitest-toothed smile I've ever seen. He grabs my hand and holds on to it while studying me, my entire body, my entire persona, as if taking me in, absorbing me. I find it a long, rather uncomfortable moment being ogled that way. By the time he has let go of my hand, I get the feeling I've passed some sort of inspection and am now a friend, a friend he cherishes.

Quentin's larger-than-life persona is as blindingly charismatic as his teeth are white. With his arm around my shoulder, he guides me to the couch. It's as if he has already accepted me, and we haven't even spoken two words.

I'd seen him before, a god of a man, at various award shows. He's tall, about six three, or four, athletic-looking with the jaunty confidence of a man of enormous power. As an added bonus, he has the unfair advantage of luxuriously thick golden hair worn Robert Redford-style. In fact, he resembles Redford with the square jaw and the piercing blue eyes.

Sitting on the edge of the couch, I take a resume from my briefcase. He puts it on his desk without looking at it.

I have my "book" (portfolio) with me. I start to open it. Quentin motions me to keep it closed. "I've seen your work."

Then he says something that scares the shit out of me: "I

think we may be able to help each other out." I have absolutely no idea what he means. "If you don't mind my saying this, and it is in no way intended as an insult, it's quite apparent that you'll never get another job in Boston—and probably not anywhere else--not after the spectacular way you managed to lose the last one with the Chagall."

Okay, if he wants to believe it was a Chagall, that's fine with me. It's like he *admires* me or something. I wait to hear what he has to say and what he has to say is unreal.

"However, if you choose to work for me, you'll have another chance in Boston, and this time you won't find yourself out on the street."

All this information is whirling around in my head. *If I choose to work for him?* It's my choice?

"The Boston office was always one of our big moneymakers," he says, "but now it's one of our biggest money losers. The good old boys up there haven't kept up with the times. A bunch of new 'boutique' agencies have popped up and are stealing our accounts left and right."

I hear all this, but at the same time, I don't hear a thing. I'm still working on what he said about *if I choose to work for him.* Those seven words swirl around and around in my head.

"I need someone who can get the place moving again. I need someone who is daring, takes risks, and can deliver. I need someone like you." Is he talking to me? I feel like looking around the room to see if someone else is standing behind me.

"The creative product is in need of a drastic change," Quentin continues. "New blood has to be brought in. A creative transformation has to happen. I'm looking for someone who'll get the ball rolling…"

I say nothing. Better that I keep my mouth shut for a change.

"Bunny Berger sent me a lot of people who were absolutely terrific. Great talents. Smart and personable, with excellent track records. These are people who would be an asset to any agency, and I rejected all of them."

He pauses a moment to see if I am taking this in, which I'm

trying my damnedest to do.

"They lacked one thing. That crazy, unique driving power that means absolutely no compromise. My spies in Boston and New York tell me you're one crazy son of a bitch who continuously puts himself on the line. That's why you've risked your reputation and your livelihood, and have been kicked out of job after job. That's what I'm looking for."

What is he talking about? Is he nuts? I want to tell him that he's way off base if he thinks I'm the character he just described. I don't even *think* when I do these things. I just do them and then pay the consequences.

I want to tell Quentin that I'm a total screw-up, someone who is scared, defensive and insecure, acting out of an ego need, so as to have some reason for even existing. On top of that, I'm dangerously irresponsible—look how I got all those innocent people fired.

Quentin is still talking. "If you take this job you'll have support for a change. I'll be there to back you up one-hundred percent. Then we'll have ourselves one fine office, yes sir."

If I take the job??

"But there are some difficult situations that come with the territory. One of them is the management," Quentin says. "Those guys should have been put out to pasture years ago." I get an "Uh-oh" message in my brain. I have never gotten along with management.

"First thing is that you have to meet the people up there. Hobart Powell is the general manager. It would be a good thing to get him on your side, not that Powell gets to vote one way or the other when it comes to hiring you. It's just a courtesy. Oh yeah, there's somebody else, Guy Ridgeley, the creative director. He's been with the agency for years and was very effective in the day when bad advertising was the all the rage."

Bad advertising? *That's all AAB does.* I don't interrupt him because of an unfortunate tendency on my part to state the obvious. In this case, what's obvious is the really appalling work coming out of New York.

But that's neither here nor there. I concentrate on what Quentin has in mind. As far as I can see, he has a plan, and wants me to help him carry it out. At least I think that's what he's saying. If I help him make a success of it, salvage the Boston office, make it flourish, I might actually have some sort of future.

The door of Quentin's office opens and Olga, Quentin's scary personal assistant, enters. "They're waiting for you in the boardroom."

"So I take it you'll consider the job?" Quentin asks.

I hesitate: "I'd have to know a little more about it," not knowing why I would say such an asinine thing.

Quentin looks at me in amazement. "What's to know? It's a great opportunity, and quite honestly, it may be your last. Is it the money?"

It isn't. I wasn't even thinking about the money. I was thinking what a fraud, I am, an absolute phony. This whole scene is surreal. To have someone actually *want* me at this stage in the game is bizarre, to my way of thinking.

"I'll give you fifty," Quentin says.

I stop him before I panic outright. I don't want that much. I don't deserve that much. Standing, I tell him I have to catch the plane back to Boston, but he won't let me go until I agree to see Powell and Ridgeley. I agree, shake his hand, and again note the seductive way he is looking at me. All I can think is: Get me out of here!

Outside, on the street, I try to feel good about what has just happened, but it's impossible because I feel nervous when things are going right. And it looks like things could definitely be going right.

On the flight back to Boston, a tall, lanky man takes the seat next to mine after tossing his Burberry raincoat (you can tell from the distinctive, tartan lining) in the bin above.

This, I realize, is Tod Lawson, Denise's disproportionately privileged and wealthy Boston Brahmin husband. He's one of those guys with millions who doesn't have to work, but does, as it turns out, as an account executive at, of all places, AAB/

Boston.

From the little I know of him, it seems he would like the world to think he's just like everybody else, an ordinary guy who lives on his salary. Which is, of course, ridiculous. The mere fact that he works at all, especially in the advertising business, is also ridiculous.

"Hi Tod," I say.

-17-

Tod, for a moment, looks blank. He obviously doesn't remember me at all, or that Denise had introduced us, Allie and me, at a children's hospital fundraiser last May.

"Bob Bronson," I say, helping him out. "You know, Denise's friend Allie's husband?"

I half expect him to draw another blank, but he now registers Allie, and also something else--the fact that he is trapped sitting next to the most infamous man in the Boston advertising community.

"Why yes," he says with jutted jaw, "You're the man who likes to *puncture* things, aren't you?"

If you live in Boston long enough, you are bound to come into contact with members of the high-born aristocracy known as Boston Brahmins. It's rarely a pleasant experience.

"Denise was just telling me about your long-suffering wife," Tod says, his tongue dripping in acid. "And how is the lovely bride?"

"Just fine, and how's yours?" I say, thinking of that living room scene with his *lovely* bride, her legs spread and my face buried in her crotch.

Now that Tod has established himself as thoroughly dislikable, I am dismissed, not worth continuing a conversation with. Opening his briefcase, he removes a folder, making it clear that our little chat is over.

"Still with AAB/Boston?" I ask, purposely intruding upon him. He's a big name there as well in Boston advertising circles because of his wealth and social contacts.

Many AAB clients—such as the managing directors at United Baby, Carlton calculators and the *Boston Times-Informer*—were classmates of his at Harvard.

Tod looks up from the report or whatever it is he's reading with a look of disdain. "And are you still…"

"A jobless vagabond?" I want to say, knowing that this is what he's labeling me, but instead, "I'm looking into a couple of things."

"Well, imagine my *relief* in knowing that," Tod says sourly. "Now if you'll excuse me…"

"In fact, I have one pretty good prospect, right in good old Boston." I'm just waiting to spring it on him that I am as good as hired in his agency.

"Is that so? I would have thought you'd be relocating to some distant city—like Addis Adaba."

"It looked like that was going to be the case," I say cheerfully, "but then this copy chief job was offered to me."

"Oh, really? And what agency, may I ask, would actually hire you?"

I'm relishing the moment. Can't wait to see his expression when I tell him.

"Well, yours, actually. Isn't that an amazing coincidence?"

Now I have his attention. "AAB/Boston?"

"None other," I say, "I've already got the job if I want it." I wait for Tod to recover.

"And whom, if you don't mind my inquiring, would have hired you?"

"Ever hear of John Quentin?"

"John Quentin, I see. And our managing director, Hobart Powell, approves?"

"Not yet," I answer. Quentin is arranging a meeting with him, as a courtesy." From my tone, it's apparent that it doesn't really matter if Hobart Powell approves or not, that Quentin does the hiring.

Frown marks now appear on Tod's face indicating the exact

effect I want. He's probably wondering about his client list of conservative fuddy-duddies and how it would look if someone as unbalanced as I've proved myself to be were to blow up again.

Could he be powerful enough to keep me out of AAB/ Bos-ton? I put that thought aside as soon as I think it. If Powell can't vote on creative staff, Tod sure as hell can't.

Tod takes a long moment to mull over this news. "I'm sur-prised that John Quentin would consider someone of your *tem-perament* for AAB/Boston."

"To tell the truth, so am I," I laugh, "but John is anxious for someone with radical ideas to completely overhaul the anti-quated AAB/Boston creative product—and thinks I can do it."

I watch Tod's face as I say this. Tiny beads of sweat have formed on his upper lip. I'm enjoying the fact that he is squirm-ing in his seat. The idea of someone like me coming in and *com-pletely overhauling the creative product* is enough to strike terror into the hearts of the ultra-conservative old guard, of which Tod is a good soldier.

"I see," Tod says before falling dead silent and taking refuge once again in his reading. Our little chat is definitely over. Tod's facial features are set in the kind of rigor mortis similar to those of his famous forebears whose portraits line the walls of the Harvard Club.

Having made my first enemy at AAB/Boston, I feel much better.

-18-

The interview Quentin has set up between me and Hobart Powell takes place two days later, in his office. My first impression of Powell is that of a kindly old gent in his early sixties, grandfatherly, fair, stalwart.

Just looking at him, I can instantly trace his line back to the Mayflower. Upstanding New England stock. Boston is full of upstanding, New England stock. Ultra-conservative, smug, clannish, and narrow.

"Well," Powell says, warmly taking both my hands in his, "you're the young man John Quentin has been praising so highly. It's a great pleasure to meet you! I'm afraid I'm rather inadequate in terms of interviewing a creative person, but our creative director, Guy Ridgeley, is in Los Angeles making commercials and I'm pinch- hitting for him."

I wonder about this. It's very unusual to be interviewed for a creative position by anyone other than the creative director. Powell motions me to a chair across from his desk, and we sit. Behind his desk is floor-to-ceiling plate glass and beyond that a staggering view of sailboats moving lazily 41 stories below on the Charles.

"John tells me that you're a topflight writer," Powell says, as if incredibly impressed. "He tells me you've won all kinds of awards and that you have enormous talent." Powell looks like he has never in his life met anyone as fascinating as me.

Usually, I can't deal with account executives, especially ones who use words like "topflight." Powell is obviously a glorified account exec--in other words, "one of them," never to be trust-ed for a moment. But he seems nice and harmless, and he's so interested in me that my guard is relaxed. Quentin must have really laid it on thick.

"Tell me a little about yourself," Powell says. As he listens, he is doodling on a pad of paper. I tell him about my "topflight" writing career—the edited version--leaving out the record-set-ting number of firings, hassles, upsets, tantrums, disasters, and especially this last episode here in Boston. I dwell, instead, on the few positives of my working life.

"You did those?' he says with an air of wonder when I rattle off the various ad campaigns I'm known for.

"And you were working on the Robert Kennedy campaign until the time of his assassination? That must have been quite an experience."

"It was. Had Kennedy lived, he would have made the kind of president this country needs. I treasure the very limited con-nection I had working on his campaign. He was really moving ahead in the polls." From Powell's non-reaction, it occurs to me that I'm talking to a Republican.

"Well, I can see why John Quentin is impressed with your work, and with you, but I have one question."

"Sure," I say, "What is it?"

"Well, it's this. I'm just curious as to why in hell John Quen-tin would send me someone with your horrendous reputation and notoriety here in Boston?"

The smile has slid off Powell's face, onto the floor. The jig is up. This bastard has been playing me along, setting me up. The change in the atmosphere has gone from warm and fuzzy to cold and clammy. It hits me that there is no way I could ever be hired into this agency.

"John Quentin obviously doesn't know how things work up here in Boston. Our clients are extremely low-key. They hate scandal of any kind. When Quentin mentioned your name as a possible candidate for the position of copy chief, I said to him, 'John, are you out of your mind?' I said this man lost an enor-

mous account for a local competitor by flagrantly displaying ut-
ter disregard for decent behavior. And you want to stick him
here?' "

Powell isn't finished. "Of course, Quentin's in charge of
pop-ulating our creative department. What he says goes. And
he seems to think that you're the man we're seeking. I would,
nev-ertheless, fight tooth and nail to prevent you from stepping
one foot into this agency."

I'm still reacting to the way Powell sprang on me, but I find my
voice. "If you feel that way, why did you agree to interview me?"

"I had no choice. If Quentin tells me to see someone, I see that
person."

"Well, you saw me, " I say, standing. "And now I'm outta
here."

"If I were you, young man, I wouldn't just get out of this office, but out of this city."

"Listen, buddy" I reply, "judging from the crap you have on
your foyer walls, and the well-known fact that you've been losing clients left and right, you would be lucky to get someone like
me. Someone who might be able to save your stuffy little outfit
here from disappearing off the face of the earth."

Powell's face grows red and he starts puffing and wheezing.

"And furthermore, grandpa, people like you are what keeps
advertising stale and musty. You should be retired and sitting in
a rocking chair somewhere."

Powell gets halfway out of his chair, but slumps back into it.
"Get out," he sputters. "Get out!"

As I pass his desk to leave, I notice what he was doodling. It's
the Star of David. Well, I know that Boston isn't a city that wel-
comes Jews, that there's quite an active prejudice against them.

It's not like New York where everyone seems Jewish. On the
plane from Boston to New York the other morning, I heard a
Roman Catholic priest talking to another priest: "Oy, such a
pain already with that trip to Boston. I had to schlepp all the
way up there to meet Archbishop Gilhooley. And for what I ask
you...just to listen to this schlumphh kvetching on and on and

on about nothing? Made me crazy."

I remember reading about a poll taken in Boston during WWII in which people were asked who they hated the most. The first were the Nazis, the second were the Japanese, and the third were Jews.

But prejudice on the part of Boston society isn't my main concern. My main concern is that I won't be able to get a job in this city and what is going to happen to Allie, the kids and me. The bills are piling up—and there are no other job prospects. I'm in big trouble.

I don't have to guess what to expect when I get to get home. Allie is waiting, hopeful and nervous.

The children are playing somewhere in the house. I hear their muted voices. Certainly the rattled nerves of their parents have had an effect on them, creating unrest in their small, un-formed minds. Allie asks how the interview went.

I take her in my arms and try to soften the blow. "He didn't like me," I tell her.

Allie regards me for a moment, and then leaves the room. "I've got to put the kids to bed."

Next day I get up early and take my book and walk around Boston, not knowing what else to do. When I get home, I call out Allie's name. I've bought her some flowers. She's not there. On the hall table, there are two messages waiting for me.

The first is that John Quentin has called several times and that I'm to call him back no matter what time of day or night.

The second message is that she has left me for good with no in-tention of ever coming back, and has taken the children with her.

-19-

I don't have the nerve to call Quentin back. I don't want to hear that, after my disastrous interview with Powell, he's changed his mind and doesn't want me in the job. I already know that.

I'm sitting in my dark living-room where I've been contemplating death. Not suicide. Two different things. Death would be peaceful, serene. Suicide would hurt and I'm too much of a coward to do such a thing. I Just wish to be out of this pain. Allie and the kids are gone. I have failed as a husband, father and provider.

Wandering through the house, I'm unable to adjust to the fact that Allie took off like that. Where did she go? We only have the one car, so she had to have arranged transportation. A taxi maybe. To the airport? And after that, where? Will she be in touch? Let me know where she went? I'm worried sick.

Maybe she's still here somewhere in Brookline. With Denise? Many of her clothes still hang in the closet. Her perfume still sits on our dresser. She forgot to take her bathrobe.

Like a sleepwalker, I continue this excursion into Angela's, Stephen's and Charlie's rooms. Their toys are scattered here and there. Their drawings are tacked up on the walls. I almost expect to see them sleeping in their beds, but their beds are empty.

I never thought Allie would walk out on me. We'd been through so much together. After re-reading her note of departure, I must have taken some time off, mentally. In other words, I don't remember late afternoon turning into evening and then night.

It's the shadowy figure of Miss Martin, our next-door neighbor, who I call "The eyes of Cypress Street," rousing me out of my amnesiac state when she appears on our veranda and rings the bell. "It's only me," Miss Martin says, "Saw your lovely wife going off with the kids this afternoon. In a station wagon, I think it was. Took some luggage with them."

I try to keep the look of dismay from creeping onto my face. She may not be able to see the dismay due to her poor eyesight, but she gets a good whiff of it.

"Something wrong?" she asks, knowing full well there is. She peers into the darkness of my doorway and then down at my hand. I am still clutching the flowers I bought for Allie about a thousand years ago this afternoon.

I thrust them at Miss Martin, who has been an old lady for a very long time and the chief source of information on Cypress Street even longer.

"Won't you have these flowers, Miss Martin?" I ask. She probably prefers to know the full details about Allie and me, but settles for the bouquet.

"Why, thank you," she says.

"What color was it?" I ask

"What color was what, Mr. Bronson."

"The station wagon. The one that picked up my wife and kids."

"Oh, that," Miss Martin says without hesitation. "It was light metallic green with a New Hampshire license plate, number MT438Y. It was driven by a blonde woman. I've seen her before. I think she's Mrs. Bronson's sister."

"Beryl!" I say.

I should have known. Beryl has been trying to get Allie to leave me for years. And I know exactly why. She was jealous of Allie because Allie had married a professional man who'd made stockpiles of money on occasion, while she was married to a petty officer in the Navy at a much lower salary. She was also jealous because she couldn't have kids, and Allie had three. I leave Miss Martin on the veranda when I hear the phone ringing. It must be Allie. It has to be Allie.

Picking up the phone, and half-sobbing, I plead into the receiver: "Allie, please come home! I love you and I need you. Please don't leave me. Please don't leave me, Pleeeeeeease don't leave meeee!" I wait for Allie's reply.

"Hey, Bob," John Quentin says, "Are you okay?"

-20-

I'm in the car driving to Portsmouth. My '68 Plymouth Satellite with its 5-litre engine practically flies.

It doesn't take long, only an eternity, and I'm in front of Beryl's white frame house. I sit in the car trying to figure out what to say to Allie. I only know one thing. I want her back.

If I imagine that's going to be easy, I'm wrong. Beryl must have heard me drive up. She spots me from an upstairs window as I sit in the car. I spot her, too, with her short, fizzled, brassy blonde hair that's always badly dyed, and her mouth that's always chewing gum and making crass remarks about me that she labels as "candid."

I wait for Beryl to tell Allie that I'm out here in the car, but apparently she has no intention of doing so, because she pulls down a shade and turns off the light. I might have to sit in the car till morning, but I get out of the car and walk toward the front door. Beryl opens it before I have a chance to ring the bell.

"Where's Allie?" I ask.

"Get lost, creep" is Beryl's loving reply.

"Do me a favor, will you, Beryl? Go tell Allie I'm here. I have some good news for her."

"What's the good news?" Beryl asks, "That you have an inoperable brain tumor and are going to die in agonizing pain?"

Beryl's husband volunteers to stay at sea for months on end and I can understand why.

"Look, Beryl, this is between Allie and me."

"And the lawyers," Beryl chirps.

"The lawyers? The lawyers for what?"

"The divorce, dummy." Beryl is enjoying this.

"What divorce?" I say, panicking. "Who wants a divorce?"

Beryl chews her gum for a moment and then, like a musician waiting for the proper beat, she lets me have it: "*We* do," she chimes.

Then I hear Allie's voice from inside the house. "Who's there?" she asks.

"It's me, Allie," I shout, afraid Beryl will slam the door in my face.

"Oh, for Pete's sake, Beryl, let him in," Allie says wearily.

"Come in, crumb," Beryl says. She steps aside, but still holds the door open.

Allie looks awful. Her hair hangs in lank layers around her face, and her clothes look like she's been sleeping in them. Her face is puffy and pale.

"What are you doing here?" she asks.

"I want you to come home. Quentin called me a couple of hours ago. I got the job!"

"I thought you said the Boston guy didn't like you." Allie says.

"He doesn't, but Quentin is the boss and he gave me the job."

As I tell Allie this, I can hardly believe the way this has turned out. When Quentin called earlier and said I had the job, I told him what had happened with Powell, and he told me to make believe it never happened. He, Quentin, was in charge and wanted me in the Boston office as the new copy chief and that that was all mattered.

Much to my amazement, he never mentioned the strange way I answered the phone.

"Well, that's just great," Allie says. "You're starting a job with a managing director who hates you. How long do you think you're going to last before you're out in the street again? A week? A month?"

"Come home with me, Allie," I say, "We can start all over again." But even as I say this I know that we both know there's a good chance nothing will change.

"No, Bobby," Allie says. "I can't do it anymore. I need a rest."

I can see that Allie needs a rest, and if that's all it is, I'll gladly let her stay, but something in her manner makes me think she meant what she scribbled on that bit of paper, that she's leaving me for good.

"You really don't intend to come home, do you?" I ask. The reality of my words catches her unawares. She hasn't had time to prepare her eyes. They tell me, in a somewhat compassionate way, that what I say is true.

"What if I say I'll change?" I ask. "I will, I'll change, I promise." Beryl starts whistling and looking up at the ceiling.

"I'm tired," Allie says, heading toward the stairs to her bedroom.

"Visiting hours are o-ver," Beryl says in a semi-falsetto.

"Allie, wait, listen to me, please."

Allie stops, turns, and faces me. "Bobby, for once in your life, give me a break."

She walks up the darkened stairway and out of sight. All that's left is the self-satisfied smirk on Beryl's gone-to-seed face, as she holds the front door open and, with a grand flourish, waves me out.

-21-

This Allie of tonight is a lot different from the confident, fun-loving, mischievous, glamorously sophisticated Allie I first knew. That's when we were two sex-crazed animals, pawing each other, waiting for any opportunity to make love.

One particular Saturday morning, coming in to the office on our own time to finish some work, we found ourselves the only occupants on the floor—the buyers were never known to work on weekends.

In the middle of working on our pages, we suddenly had to have each other. We decided that Dunfrey's office, three times larger than ours, would be the ideal place to make love.

There, on Dunfrey's deep-pile carpet, we spent a considerable amount of time pleasuring each other and then, walking back to our office, Allie naked from the waist down, slacks tossed casually over one shoulder, we bumped into Mr. Hurd, one of the buyers, who had unexpectedly come in to do some work.

"Good afternoon, Mr. Hurd," Allie said pleasantly, strolling into our office, not at all perturbed. "Lovely day, isn't it?"

Mr. Hurd, a tall, florid man of about fifty, said nothing. He just stopped and stared at us, as if unable to believe what he was seeing.

"Well, that's the end of us," I said, once our door was closed. "He's sure to tell Dunfrey' and we'll be canned."

"Don't be silly, darling," Allie said. "Nothing will happen."

"How do you know nothing will happen?" I asked.

"Because even if Daryl Hurd did say anything, who would believe him?"

Allie was right. She was often right. But she was dead wrong about one thing: She should have married Beau Bennett.

-22-

If I'd been waved out of Beryl's house with all the nastiness and venom of a rattlesnake, I'm welcomed at AAB in exactly the opposite manner by, of all people, Hobart Powell. There he stands in the reception area, wearing a smile as cheerful as his polka-dot bow tie.

He's the model of politeness and diplomacy as he escorts me, like I was an important dignitary, out of the reception area and into the interior of the agency.

"Bob," he says, as if the unpleasant scene of a few days before never occurred, "welcome to our little family at Abbott, Ayler, Ballard. We are pleased to have you aboard." Certain older admen of the establishment-type often use that "welcome aboard"—as if they are Rear Admirals.

I'm puzzled by Powell's friendly demeanor—is he suffering from dementia like Dr. Perlberg? What happened to the vindictive bastard of the other day?

"How was the journey in?" he asks. It's hardly what you would call a journey from Brookline Village, just four miles. But by the way he asks, you'd think I'd traveled from Antarctica to get here.

"Fine," I say.

I almost miss the Powell I originally met. His sugary sweetness of today is hard to take.

"Good. Very good. Excellent, in fact. Let me give you a tour of the creative department and to show you to your office. We hope you will settle in easily and find everything to your liking.

We want you to be very comfortable indeed."

I don't know about being made comfortable, but I know what's making me damned uncomfortable and that's the fact I haven't met Guy Ridgeley, the creative director. There's no sign of him. We walk down a long hall, the walls of which are lined with framed ads that Ridgeley is responsible for.

There isn't one I would have ever put my name to. They're staid, corny, and full of the consumer-is-an-idiot jargon that gives advertising a bad name. But at the same time, each one is glossy and expensively-produced: glossy, expensively-produced crap.

I think of agencies I've worked for in New York where, if I'd presented any of these terrible concepts to my bosses, I would have been canned on the spot. Still, I'm not all that bothered that this agency has done such dreck in the past—because from now on, I'm determined to change all that. I am aware that it's going to be a challenge trying to introduce innovative, honest advertising to personnel who wouldn't know it if it bit them.

Farther down the corridor, we reach what must be the creative row. Copywriters and art directors in their individual offices are peering out, studying, openly assessing, taking in and dissecting me; no doubt wondering what kind of copy chief I will be.

I can almost hear the thoughts racing through their heads: Will my arrival signal a whole new regime? Will I demand great work from them? Will they be capable of delivering great work that will meet with my approval? Will they have to worry about keeping their jobs? Will they have to start thinking of what other agencies might hire them if they have to leave here? Will I be impossible to deal with and a pain in the ass?

They'll have heard of me—who in Boston hasn't? They'll know my entire life story for that matter—my age, where I was born, what ads and theme lines I'm known for, how many awards I've won, how many agencies I've worked for since the start of my career and in what capacity. They'll know, of course, how I destroyed, as the now mythical story goes, a 'real' Chagall, and how I got so many people fired in my last agency.

I don't blame them for being apprehensive. The hiring of any new department head is sure to cause trepidation. Any new leader is sure to bring about bothersome change.

Powell shows me into a spacious office with a window looking down on the Sheraton Hotel, 41 stories down. There's even a sliver of the Charles River—if you stand in exactly the right spot while squinting.

After introducing me to my secretary, a pretty blonde by the name of Sondra, Powell mentions Ridgeley for the first time. "When Guy returns from Los Angeles, where he's making and editing commercials for our Biggah Frozen Foods account, you will, of course, report directly to him."

So Ridgeley does exist. Does he know I exist? That I've been hired? Proper protocol would have been for me to have my initial interview with him instead of Powell. Why was he kept out of the picture?

In Boston's gossipy, backbiting, cattily-vicious advertising community, Guy isn't exactly thought of as a creative force. It's rare that he wins an award for his creative output. The agency itself, doing very safe, very boring old-fashioned work, isn't one that garners awards.

Though I've never met Ridgeley, I can tell from the sorry state of the creative product that he's more account executive than creative director. A corporate clown. So I'm not fooling myself about what's going to happen when he returns to the agency. He'll want to hang on to the same old stale brand of advertising, while I'll be pushing for innovation. There is sure to be conflict, maybe even bloodshed.

Powell leaves me to settle into my new office, but not before grabbing both my hands again, assuring me that he will do everything, absolutely everything in his power to help make my tenure a rousing success.

Yeah, right. An hour later, an inter-agency memo lands on my desk. It's written by Powell and addressed to all AAB/Boston personnel for the express purpose of introducing me as AAB's current copy chief.

Maybe I'm over-sensitive, but "*current*" jumps off the page. It may as well say "temporary." If I think Powell has become docile in any way, I am sadly mistaken as time will prove.

-23-

The first thing I do as AAB's "current" copy chief is to call a morning session with my writers. Then, because of an incident on the way to work, I almost miss my own meeting.

All civilian traffic is stopped when an army convoy passing through downtown Boston on the way to the Mass Turnpike is met by several dozen anti-war protestors, who sit down in the path of the trucks.

Our troops are seen by some Americans as traitors. They are cursed, ridiculed, and sometimes physically attacked. Many don't dare wear their uniforms when on leave or liberty for fear of being targeted by irate protestors. But you can always tell a serviceman by his close-cropped hair—so different from the long hairstyles for men that came about with the Beatles.

I sympathize with those fighting this dumb war. Having served in the Marines myself, I can sense the sting these guys must be feeling, the feeling of exclusion from society.

Speaking of exclusion, I get a strong whiff of that myself when I finally arrive at the office. It's coming from just about everyone in the copy department, especially Kyle Knas and Chaney Ferncliff. They sit there in the conference room staring at me as if contemplating my demise. It's okay, because I am *definitely* planning theirs.

These are, without a doubt, the two worst copywriters I've ever encountered, the ones responsible for most of the dreadful work in the reception area. I can imagine them kissing up to Ridgeley and Powell, having them as allies, which is all the more reason they have to go.

The other two, Healy Derekson and Julie Ash are both extremely talented writers, the ones I want to keep no matter what. They're not much friendlier. Healy barely looks me in the eye. He's a small-framed cockney, the kind of London East-Ender you imagine selling fish and chips on a corner, but his credentials are impeccable. They include the prestigious Collett, Dickenson, Pearce In London, reputed to be the best agency in the world.

Julie, like me, is a transplant from New York where she worked at an agency that really *is* the best in the world, Doyle, Dane, Bernbach.

I now realize I have heard of her before. Who in Boston hasn't? It's not every day you have a real live Hungarian countess working in the advertising business.

The story goes, she and her aristocratic family fled Hungary after the uprising against Russia in 1956, and settled on Park Avenue in New York. In a newspaper interview, she played down her countess status and talked of dropping out of college in her freshman year to pursue the only career she desired, and that was to write in a large ad agency.

Apparently, she eats, sleeps and breathes the business, but what I can't figure out is why someone with her talent and devotion to good advertising would work in a place that has practically banned it. And in backwater Boston of all places.

Maybe for the same reason as me. Maybe she outdid her welcome in New York. Who knows. But for now, I count myself lucky, as would any quality-driven creative director or copy chief new to an agency, in having her and Healy. And I aim to keep them. If that means taking their shit for the present time, so be it. I just hope the countess and the cockney won't take jobs at some other agency and leave me stranded with the deadly duo, Knas and Ferncliff.

I can't worry about that right now. Job orders are already flying into my office from the frenzied "traffic managers" who snap the whip to keep everything running on schedule.

There's no point in including Knas or Ferncliff in the talent pool because I plan to fire them as soon as possible. I ignore them completely and concentrate on Derek and Julie who, from their non-response, indicate that they have absolutely no interest in anything I am saying.

The four faces before me are set in stone. I try, and fail, to articulate a message of enthusiasm for the work we will do in the future. The atmosphere in the room is so daunting I'm not even sure what I'm saying. I'm in a fog, confused, tongue-tied. This has turned nightmarish.

Finally, after about fifteen minutes, I can see that trying to get through to these folks is futile. I attempt one last ploy to at least reach the two talented writers. "We're going to make this the best damned creative department in the city." I'm embarrassed as to how feeble this comment sounds. There's at least one full, excruciating minute of silence right after I've uttered it. One by one the writers leave, never looking in my direction.

-24-

My life is now the agency. All the things a normal person does—eating, sleeping, relaxing—are rare occurrences for me. I get to the agency before anyone else, work right through the day and long after everyone has left. I go home, eat something to stay alive, go to bed, get up, and start the routine all over.

Being the copy chief of a busy ad agency, I find myself in a continuous, frantic, non-stop race to meet deadlines, but I refuse to compromise the quality of an ad because somebody wants it yesterday.

This brings about the first real friction I have with Powell, who couldn't care less about the quality of an ad and who has no idea what it takes to do an outstanding one. He has an account executive's mentality that's as far away from the creative brain as one can get.

"Since you've been here, things have been taking far too long and I just can't have that," Powell complains about a week after I have arrived. Gone is the friendly demeanor he displayed when I first arrived.

"Sorry you feel that way." I say. In all actuality, I don't give a damn what Powell feels.

I know there are going to be more scenes like this with Powell. He obviously never got over the fact that Quentin ignored his protests about me. The overly-polite gent who greeted me the first day is now a ferret-eyed, grim-faced, bad-tempered old shit who seems determined to make a fuss about everything.

Just as Quentin ignored him, I do the same, even yawn in his face. As long as Quentin has my back, I just concentrate on the job I'm here to do, which is to create the best goddamn advertising not only in Boston, but anywhere and everywhere.

I have a steady diet of reviewing concepts and headlines in conjunction with the visuals created by the art directors. Then based on the merits of the resultant work, I can give a copywriter/art director team the green light to go ahead and write the body copy and prepare the visual for a client presentation.

If the work they've shown me is not of an award-winning caliber, or is off-target, or is not mind-bogglingly brilliant, their task is to go away and come back again with something that is.

Eventually, and sometimes after many attempts, there will be an approval, first by me, and ultimately the creative director (in theory, the absent Guy Ridgeley), who can flush whatever I've approved down the toilet if he so wishes.

Then there are the endless meetings with the account, production, marketing, and research people.

The latter will try to dictate the direction a campaign should follow. For example, say when our ice cream account is being discussed, they'll go on and on *ad nauseam* about the emotional implications of eating the stuff.

We all know ice cream is a comfort food, rather than nutritious. It's eaten like there's no tomorrow by a ravenous public. It takes research people to tell us that?

Good writers and art directors seem to have a sixth sense that gives their work the edge in reaching the public. Julie and Healy have it. The long-haired, mustachioed and tattooed art director Nelson Tanner has it, despite or maybe due to his obvious drug addiction. Art director Rick Baxter, from Dorchester, one or Boston's roughest neighborhoods, has it with lots to spare. Art directors Vic Santoro and Ryan Phipps definitely do not have it and are in the same category as Ferncliff and Knas. Awful.

It goes without saying that I have it. I'm not required to create ads, but I love doing it. Not that I get much opportunity. With all my other responsibilities it's gotten so that I don't even get out for lunch most days.

Clearing up a pile of papers before leaving late one night, I discover a tuna salad sandwich on rye Sondra ordered for me the day before, that I never had a chance to eat.

The merciful thing about being bound to the job is that I don't have much time to think about my beloved Allie and kids.

When I do have time, it's at home after work. I miss them every minute of the evening and have an almost bone-crunching feeling of loneliness and loss and foreboding.

-25-

The foreboding manifests early one morning in the form of a phone call. I'm about to hear something that could really screw up my chances of success at AAB/Boston.

"He knows about us," a female voice says.

I have no idea who is on the other end, and then I do know. After a few seconds, I recognize that it's voice of Denise Lawson, but her cryptic message makes no sense.

"Who knows about us?" I ask.

"Who do you think?" Denise says. "My husband."

Just what I need, Tod Lawson knowing that Denise and I had a sexual encounter, disastrous as it was.

"How, Denise," I ask, does he know about us?"

"He knows because I told him."

Tod is already an arch-enemy of mine, and now this.

"Denise, why on Earth would you do such a thing?"

"I told him because he's my husband and I love him and he had to know."

"Well, he might be your husband, Denise, and you might love him, and you might have thought he had to know, Denise, but dammit, I have to work with the guy and this isn't going to make working with him an easy thing to do, Denise!"

"How is that my fault?" she says.

I don't believe this woman. She's either dense or…dense.

"The next thing I know, Denise, is that you'll be giving a scoop to the *New York Times*."

"No need to be rude," Denise says before slamming the phone down.

An hour later, there he is, as expected, Tod Lawson, standing in my doorway. "Well, you certainly do get around, don't you?" he asks. "I had originally thought I might sock you on the jaw. He sounds like a someone in a Noel Coward play where the characters are all civilized and sophisticated and talk like that. "But then I decided that perhaps I owe you a debt of gratitude for allowing me to establish grounds for divorce."

"So you are going to divorce Denise?" I ask.

"It's very probable, and of course you will be named in the suit."

Just what I need, a court wrangle. Unfavorable publicity and Allie finding out about it.

"Couldn't I just have the sock on the jaw instead?" Now I'm sounding like Noel Coward, myself.

"And spoil all the fun? Not a chance," Tod answers. "But wait, maybe I won't have to go to those extremes. Perhaps we could settle all this if you were to accommodate me in one little thing.

"And what would that be, Tod?"

"That would be for you to resign from AAB/Boston immediately. After all, you can see how awkward it would be for the two of us to work in the same agency."

I need this situation like I need a hole in the head. He wants me to quit and probably never work again for the rest of my life.

"I would make it a bit easier for you to leave here, say with a check for $25,000?"

"Very generous, Tod," I say, "but there's something I don't understand."

"And what's that, may I ask?"

"Well, it's just this, Tod: Why offer me all this money when there are so many others all over Boston and the rest of New England, not to mention New York, London and Rome that Denise has fucked. Did Denise tell you about them, too? And if she did, why don't you go after them?"

I've hit the intended nerve. The expression on Tod's face can't be mistaken for anything other than homicidal rage. Suddenly, all this gentlemanly Noel Coward banter comes to an halt.

"You've asked for it!" Tod shouts, "I'm going to teach you a lesson."

"Be my guest," I say, not thinking he'd be so stupid as to get violent. "Then maybe we can get back to work around here."

Almost instantly, I know I'm wrong. Tod goes nuts and comes after me. We're in a clinch with him trying to lift his arms to strangle me, me holding them tight against his sides so that can't happen.

We're dancing around like this, doing a grotesque polka when my secretary, Sondra, opens the door and stops in her tracks, mouth dropping open. She watches us, fascinated.

"Well, pardon me, you two," she says. "When will I learn to knock?"

Suddenly, the fight goes out of Tod. I let go and he staggers out the door and down the hall.

"What was *that* all about?" Sondra asks, and watches him wander out of sight.

"I don't know. Must have been something I said."

-26-

I'm thinking about the $25,000 Tod offered me (and how casually I turned it down) when Al Marino, cigar-chomping head of the traffic department comes in. Since I've been in this job, I've been curious about Melvin Bayers, the previous copy chief, who committed suicide.

"Hauled his typewriter through the hermetically sealed window right behind you, blew out the glass, and plunged right after it," Al tells me, "and it was bye-bye, Melvin."

It's creepy. A man with whom he worked daily on a daily basis in such desperation that he jumped 41 stories to his death, and Al is joking about it.

Also creepy is the habit Hobart Powell has made of appearing in my office doorway at various intervals. He doesn't say anything, just stands there. When I become aware of him, I ask if there is anything I can do for him, but he just smiles and walks off. One day, he actually enters my office and hands me a sheaf of papers. "Complete these before you leave tonight," No please or thank you. I look at the papers. They are like job applications in which a person gives all sorts of information. The idea is for me to report all previous jobs and my reasons for leaving them. In other words, Powell wants me to commit professional suicide.

"Why do you want to know all this?" I ask.

"All our employees above a certain salary are required to provide their past employment histories," Powell says. "In that way we   determine whether they deserve to work for us." My work record reads like a corporate disaster rap sheet. He thinks I'm going to supply the evidence to hang myself?

"You should have asked for this information before I was hired," I say, shoving the papers back to him.

"Nevertheless," Powell says, shoving them back, "I expect the papers filled out by the end of the work day."

"Fat chance, Hobart," I think.

"And another thing." He says. "We have a dress code around here in case you didn't know it. This includes the wearing of neckties at all times whether to a client meeting or in the office. You have violated this code continually with your open-neck shirts and I've noticed that some of the people in your department have now adopted your slovenly way of dressing."

I just let Powell make a lot of noise about this. I always wear a tie at client meetings, and that's enough as far as I'm concerned, seeing that I hate ties. In some New York agencies, the tie has been banished forever. I've even considered wearing jeans to the office. Now that would really be outrageous, and just might drive Powell out of his mind.

My nonconformist way of dressing isn't the main reason for Powell's dislike of me. I think the real reason is his hatred of all things Jewish. How do I know this for sure? For one thing there are no Jewish execs in the agency. White, Anglo-Saxon Protestants make up the population in most departments, certainly in the account and research departments.

When I won't submit my past employment records to Powell or dress in the way he demands, he comes up with something so totally amazing that I can't help but admire his genius for complete corporate lunacy.

He has called an evening strategy meeting to determine the direction and future of the agency. On the invitation list are all the AAB/Boston department heads, as well as all the account execs as well, even the junior account execs. Glaringly, there is one name he's left off the list.

Which just so happens to be mine.

-27-

You would think that instead of trying to frustrate me into quitting, Powell would be grateful that someone is taking care of this impossible workload so efficiently, especially when the person most responsible for the creative product, namely the creative director, Guy Ridgeley, hasn't been around or even heard from in all the time I've been copy chief. But that's about to change.

One Monday morning, as I'm waiting for an elevator, I notice a slim, elegantly dressed man sweep through the revolving doors as if he owns the building. Following him is a young cherubic-looking black man herding two gigantic French poodles.

"If you can't get up in the morning, you have no business being my assistant," the older man says as he approaches the elevator banks. Up close, I see he has one of those sculpted faces with high cheekbones and prematurely silver hair expertly styled.

"The alarm clock didn't go off," the young man replies.

"The alarm clock didn't go off," the older man mocks, pressing the elevator button with a beautifully manicured index finger.

"I've never known anyone who is so consistently late. Perhaps I should look around for somebody who has enough sense to set the clock the night before so that it will go off in the morning, someone who can be relied upon."

"Look," the young man says, "you hired me to be your personal assistant, not your chauffeur and dog-sitter."

"Are you complaining, Abraham?" the older man snaps. "Because if you are, I can give somebody else the same, golden opportunity I gave you, and I might at least get some gratitude out of it."

To escape the wrath of the older man, the younger one walks about twenty yards for a drink at the water fountain, at which time the elevator arrives. I get in with the elegant gent who lets the doors close without waiting for the younger man.

"Shouldn't we wait?" I ask. I see he has pressed the same floor as me. I idly wonder what business he has up there.

"No," he says, looking through me, rather than at me, "Let him take the next car. He had me waiting long enough this morning, a full hour. He's never on time. I tell you, taking these people out of the jungle is a thankless task. Here I give him the job of a lifetime and gamble that this one will be different from the rest of his race, and what do I get?"

It's quite apparent what he gets: A latter-day slave.

"And here I am," he continues, "just back from the most God-awful month of my life only to be met with this kind of grief. Makes me wonder what he's been up to while I've been gone. Well, we shall soon find out, shant we?"

"Where have you been?" I ask conversationally, but get no answer. I repeat my question, this time a little louder.

"Huh? Oh, the west coast, shooting commercials."

It hits me like a major newsflash. This is Guy Ridgeley, creative director of AAB/Boston.

-28-

Well, Ridgeley and I were going to meet someday. I just didn't know it was going to be in an elevator, and I certainly didn't know that I was going to be the one to introduce him to his new copy chief. If it were me finding out that my copy chief had been hired by someone else, I'd resign on the spot.

Maybe Ridgeley will do the same. Any way you look at it, he is sure to lose face, as well as the respect of just about everybody in the creative department, not to mention the entire agency. And what can he do about it?

If he chooses not to confront it, he'll have to smile the embarrassment away. Smile when someone makes a comment or crack about my being hired by Quentin, and not him, smile when people snicker behind his back as they will. Smile when the ad community of Boston treats him like a eunuch.

The humiliation is enough to destroy anyone, especially Ridgeley, who is already on shaky ground when it comes to his creative output. I anticipate a very awkward scene when Ridgeley discovers who I am and that I'm in the process of reorganizing the copy department so that it will run efficiently for a change.

I wonder what excuse Ridgeley will fabricate to explain a new copy chief that he himself did not hire. Maybe he "was busy and asked Powell and Quentin to find someone." No one, in a million years, will believe that whopper, but it just might get him through this tough period so that he can recover some of his pride.

Why do I care? I have no idea. I just don't like to see anyone

CHARLES RUBIN

kicked in the teeth.

In anticipation of my possible clash with Ridgeley, I just hope Powell has mentioned my existence.

The elevator doors open on the 41st floor and Ridgeley and I step out. All of a sudden, know Powell hasn't mentioned me. *The son of a bitch wants us to clash! He wants there to be a war between us and then to claim that I am the reason!*

Timidly, I follow Ridgeley into the reception area. He seems like a scary character with a tongue that can slash you to pieces and render you a babbling idiot.

"May I help you?" he asks, as we walk down the same hall. Maybe he thinks I'm lost.

"No thanks," I answer, "I'm just going to my office."

"Your office? You mean you work here? Gracious me, how things do happen when one is away," Ridgeley says, lighting a cigarette. "But you're on the wrong floor. The account and media departments are on the 40th floor and broadcasting is on 39. Which one do you work for?"

"Neither, uh__"

"Well, then research? They're on 38. Don't tell me they've finally decided to get their act together. That is the worst department in the agency."

"Actually, I'm in the creative department," I say, plunging right in and holding my breath until my words burrow into Ridgeley's brain.

"You're in the *what?*" Ridgeley asks, his eyes widening like Joan Crawford's in the movie *Mildred Pierce*, when she finds out that her lover, Zachary Scott, is cheating on her with her daughter, Ann Blyth.

"Uh, the creative department," I say.

Suddenly, Ridgeley turns on me. "What the hell do you mean the creative department? Who the hell are you and how the hell did you get into my department? And what the hell is going on here?"

It's true then, Powell has said nothing to him about me.

"Maybe I better introduce myself," I say, speaking with a deliberate calmness I do not ordinarily possess. I'm thinking, hoping, praying, that once I mention my name, everything will fall into place for Ridgeley, that maybe, just maybe, either Quentin or Powell will have informed him of my existence.

"I'm Bob Bronson," I say.

"Bob Bronson?" Ridgeley repeats, his face a blank. "Am I supposed to know who Bob Bronson is?"

"John Quentin contacted me."

"John Quentin?" Ridgeley asks, his voice noticeably rising, "what about John Quentin?"

"Well, he..."

"He what?"

"Well, he hired me as..."

"Wait, I don't get this...he hired you? As what?"

"Well...as copy chief," I say, thinking that at any moment I might throw up on Ridgeley's shoes.

-29-

This is one of those times when there is such a feeling of incredulity in the atmosphere, not to mention acute embarrassment, that your breathing stops and you're pretty sure that was your life that just flew before your eyes.

Ridgeley looks at me in astonishment, taking a long, theatrical drag on his cigarette and then, after a long pause: "You mean to tell me they haven't offered you the job of creative director?" he asks, his eyes widening to the max as two plumes of smoke, like those from a dragon about to devour you, exit his nostrils.

This time the resemblance is to Bette Davis, when she finds out that Anne Baxter is going to be her understudy in the classic *All About Eve.*

"I can see you're surprised," I offer, "and I don't blame you..."

"Well, isn't that nice," Ridgeley snipes. "You can see I'm surprised, and you don't blame me," he mimics. "You sneak in here while I'm gone and now you see I'm surprised and you don't blame me."

"Maybe if you could see my work, I would be the person you would hire."

"Doubtful, extremely doubtful," Ridgeley says, and then suddenly he is studying me. "Aren't you the nutcase who destroyed some client's Chagall?"

"That's what people say," I answer, no longer saying it isn't true.

"Lovely, not only have you been forced on me, but you're screwy. Well, since you are in my employ, you can follow me to my office. That is, if I still *have* an office."

Ridgeley's office is at the exact opposite end of the agency as Powell's and just as large. As we enter, there's a smell of rotting vegetation, which turns out to be a large vase of flowers, long dead, sitting on Ridgeley's desk

"Hmmm, an omen," Ridgeley says. He gingerly removes the flowers and dumps them in the wastepaper basket just as his young assistant enters the room with the poodles.

"Still thirsty?" Ridgeley asks, holding out the vase of putrid water.

I have to credit the young man who just stands there with no particular expression on his face. Even that type of non-expression on a black face might be interpreted as uppity by a white man in this day and age.

The fact that there are no black people that I know of in the very white ad agencies of New York or Boston, (other than the people who come in at night to clean), makes this guy something of a pioneer.

"Abraham," Ridgeley says, "this is our new copy chief, what did you say your name was?"

"Bob Bronson, and it still is," I reply, nodding at Abraham whose nod back is laced with a subtle but obvious opinion that his boss is to be humored.

"Imagine my astonishment, Abraham," Ridgeley says, "in finding that this person, called Bob Bronson has been hired as my copy chief without my knowing anything about it. Might it be that perhaps you had wind of this during my absence?"

"I only know one thing," Abraham says, "that old Melvin jumped out of the window, crashed through the Sheraton atrium ceiling during lunch-hour and barely missed a party of flower-club ladies. That's forty-one stories he fell. Left him looking like Sheraton's famous squash medley."

"Okay, enough of your flowery description," Ridgeley says. "Haven't you some chores to attend to at your desk?"

"That boy," Ridgeley says after Abraham has gone, "He's supposed to be my personal assistant, but he wants to be a copywriter."

"We can use a junior copywriter," I say.

"Oh, I see. You are hired behind my back and now you want to steal my assistant," Ridgeley snaps.

"I just thought…"

"Now just you listen, Bob Bronson, or whatever your name is. You were put in your job by John Quentin who sits in his ivory tower in New York thinking he knows what our clients need and want. He obviously thinks a flashy writer like you is the way to go. But he's dead wrong. We're a very conservative bunch up here in Boston."

I can see that Ridgeley is going to be giving me a hard time at every opportunity, so I may as well drop the timid act and let him know that this person called Bob Bronson can be someone to contend with.

"Guess that's why he hired me," I say purposely. "To shake things up."

"And with a cocky attitude like that, you may just shake yourself out of a job," Ridgeley says.

"Wouldn't be the first time," I say as I walk out the door.

-30-

Almost immediately after meeting Ridgeley, he has swung into high gear defending his position as creative director of AAB/Boston. He wants to see every single piece of copy presented to me by the writers, most of which he routinely rejects, and he insists on being the only creative department voice in client meetings.

Such a meeting is slated to begin in the projection room as soon as the Tummy-Lite client shows up. Ridgeley makes it quite clear he wants no interference from me. "I shall present," he says, "and you are to keep your words to a minimum."

"Aye-aye, sir," I say.

This meeting has been called because of a Tummy-Lite TV spot Healy wrote and shot here in Boston when Ridgeley was in Los Angeles. Nikki Wasserman, the mouthy broadcast producer assigned to that project, complains that the Tummy-Lite client is a schmuck.

Everything about Nikki makes an irreverent statement. Her attire—or lack of it—consists of a bikini top over a low-slung sarong skirt with a slit up the leg and crazy platform heels a la Carmen Miranda from the 1940s. Over her shoulders lies a ratty-looking, long-dead fox fur piece that she always wears.

"His problem," she explains, "besides the one he has with his inability to understand a fucking thing about making a commercial, is that the he doesn't like the voiceover we chose for this spot. But Healy, Bob and I say the voice is perfect."

"For your information," Ridgeley says, his eyebrows arching,

"I couldn't care less what Healy or Bob or you like. It's what the client likes that matters."

"Yeah, well, if you want to agree with that asshole and fuck up a good commercial, go right ahead."

Nikki, not attached to the creative department, can say what she pleases without censor from Ridgeley. She has her say just as the client and his entourage are being shown into the screening room. They barely miss her diatribe.

Ridgeley greets the client like a long-lost brother asking him about his family and whether he's been on the golf course recently. The client obviously knows Nikki and Healy, but doesn't acknowledge them.

When Ridgeley fails to introduce me, I do it myself. I get a mere grunt in reply. From the client's facial expression, I would say he regards all creative people like a bunch of radical-hippie weirdoes intent on destroying the country. It's a wonder he signed off on such a brilliant spot.

Still wearing the smarmed-on smile for his "long-lost brother," Ridgeley's eyes narrow at my impertinence. Turning to the client, he suggests we view the rough cut and then discuss the "voiceover problem." He motions to the projectionist to start the film.

The lights dim, and on screen, a short, chubby middle-aged sultan appears. He is surrounded by adoring harem girls who cater to his every wish. Some lay at his feet, others cool him with big feather fans and others dance around him.

The sultan is enjoying the attention of the girls when, all of a sudden, he grasps his stomach in pain and says he has to leave. The girls don't want him to go, but he says he has to, bids them goodbye, and rushes off.

We then cut, which in film parlance means to abruptly end one scene and go on to the next. We now see that the sultan is not a sultan at all, but an ordinary guy in bed next to an ordinary-looking sleeping wife. He might be in Pittsburgh or Detroit. The harem sequence was just a dream.

The guy is suffering from indigestion. As a matter of fact,

that's what woke him out of his dream. He gets out of bed, goes to the bathroom, and pops a Tummy-Lite tablet into a glass of water just as the voiceover starts his spiel: "Indigestion can wreck the greatest of occasions, but it takes only one Tummy-Lite tablet to remedy the situation."

The man drinks the fizzy solution, gets back into bed and immediately resumes his dream with the harem girls. "So whereja go, Sultan honey?" a gum-chewing harem girl asks. The spot ends with the final voiceover sell, and then the lights come on and Ridgeley takes the floor again.

"We understand your concern with the current voiceover choice," he says obsequiously, "and if you're not happy with it, we're not happy with it, either. To that end, we've come up with a selection of alternate voiceovers for you to choose from."

"Selection?" the client interjects. "Who the hell asked for a selection of alternate voiceovers? I asked for one voiceover. One voiceover to replace this poor excuse for a voiceover you got now."

"Understood," Ridgeley says, "but we wanted to get your input as to the kind of voiceover you feel would best benefit your product. And just to show you how much we value your business, we are not charging you for the additional hours and extra expense we've put into this."

"Goddamn right you're not," the client says. "I asked for one voiceover and that's all I'm paying for. Now enough of this bull-shit. Just play me the new voice, okay? I ain't got all day."

Nikki rolls her eyes as she turns on the tape machine. Not five words come out of it before I realize, with a jolt, that this is the very same voiceover currently on the TV spot, the very same voiceover the client hates.

For some reason it was left on the tape. I motion to Nikki to go to the next voice, but before she can do that, the client says "now that's some voiceover! I love that voiceover! That voiceover is perfect. That's the voiceover I want".

I know what's coming next and try to close my ears as Nikki announces to the client "That's the very same voiceover currently on the spot, the voiceover you said you hate."

There is a sharp intake of breath in the room that is not let out again. Nikki has broken a cardinal rule in advertising, which is to avoid, at all costs, making a client look like an idiot. Even if he is an idiot, as so many clients are.

Just the week before we'd taken a client for a dinner cruise on the Boston Harbor and he'd gotten so drunk that he fell off the boat. We fished him out and took him, soaking wet, to a bar on the wharf. We sat him up on a stool, and watched as a puddle of water formed at his feet while he had four or five more drinks. And we never said a word about him being wet. We were observing the rule of never embarrassing a client. Unlike today.

Right now, in the Tummy-Lite meeting, there is nothing but deafening silence and unrelenting tension. The minions don't know where to look—certainly not at their boss. He, meanwhile, has turned beet red and knows he has just been labeled by everyone in the room, even his own entourage, as a complete nitwit.

Ridgeley looks stricken and is muttering something about how easy it is to make a mistake, and that all voiceovers sound like one another, and how a voice on tape sounds different from a voice on a TV spot. Nothing he says eases the situation. His efforts to restore the client's confidence crash all around him.

I look over at Nikki. She has turned her back so no one can tell she is shaking with muffled laughter.

"Would you like to hear the other voices?" Ridgeley timidly asks, but the client and his bunch are out of their seats and out the door. None of the entourage talks to their boss. No one dares. He is alone in his state of acute humiliation.

Ridgeley follows the group down the hall to the elevators, cajoling them, to no effect.

Nikki has the last word. "Looks like our choice for voiceover is approved," she says. "He said he loved it."

-31-

I'm in Quentin's office a week after the Tummy-Lite fiasco. He's called me to come down to discuss a few things.

"I hear you've been annoying the hell out of Powell, Ridgeley and Lawson," Quentin says, a serious look on his Hamptons-tanned face. "Powell calls me at least twice a day complaining that you can't handle the job, can't get along with Ridgeley, that you are unfair to some of the writers, and the list goes on and on."

"Well, it must be true then" I say sarcastically. "Powell can go fuck himself for all I care. We're giving him great work and all he does is complain. Fuck him. And if you want to fire me, go right ahead. I'm ready to walk out anyway."

I never know when I'm going to shoot my mouth off. This is the story of my life in the ad business. I suddenly get into a rage about something and make a big fuss, sometimes over nothing.

"Hold hard," Quentin says. "I'm not saying I believe the son of a bitch. And I'm not saying I want to fire you. Hell, I would say you are the one person I can count on around here. But what's all this about the radio commercial?"

"What radio commercial?"

"The one Powell and Ridgeley are screaming about. The one you guys wrote for the *Boston Times-Informer*."

"We wrote six for them. Which one is he screaming about?"

"The one about the dog."

"The dog? It hasn't even been presented to the client. Ridgeley and Powell and that twit Tod Lawson wouldn't allow it at the presentation."

"Well, presented or not, he sent down the demo tape you made of it, accompanied by a comment that you are a threat to all the clients up there."

I watch as Quentin switches on the tape player. The demo begins:

Man: "Honey, have you seen the *Times-Informer* financial section anywhere?"

Woman: "The puppy's got it..."

Man: "The puppy's got it? The puppy's got the *Times-Informer* financial section???"

Woman: "Well, yesterday, I was housetraining him so I gave him the lifestyle section and he didn't...didn't...you know... go...so I thought if I gave him the *Times-Informer* financial section maybe..."

Man (annoyed): "Great! You go out and buy this intellectual dog and then give him my financial section. Well, since he's spending so much time with the Wall Street crowd, he should be able to make some interesting predictions. Hey, Ruggles, should I buy Blue Sun shares?"

Dog: Barks.

Man: "What about Transatlantic Amalgamated?"

Dog: Whines.

Man (convinced): "Well, I'll be..."

Woman: "See, I told you Ruggles was smart. Oh, by the way, he's through with the financial section...but you won't want it now..."

I look over at Quentin who's laughing. "Wait a minute," he says. "The dog takes a dump on the product?"

"That's right."

"Well, no wonder Powell and Ridgeley are complaining. They've got good reason. We could lose the client presenting a commercial like that. It says we don't respect these people or their paper."

"So go ahead and kill it," I say, not being able to contain my anger.

"Kill it? Are you crazy? It's a winner. A dog taking a dump on their paper. I love it. It's what I hired you for."

"Powell and Ridgeley try to get me canned for coming up with it and you're loving it. And you think the *Times-Informer* people will actually buy it?"

"They will."

"How can you be sure?"

"Because I'm calling the editor of the paper, a guy I know personally, and am clearing the path for you."

What I say next comes popping out of my mouth "The same way you cleared the path for me with Ridgeley?"

Quentin is taken aback by my remark. "What do you mean?"

"I'll spell it out for you, John. Ridgeley is the fucking creative director of the Boston agency and he didn't know I was hired. I had to tell him myself. And that wasn't something I especially enjoyed."

Since I have now stepped into even further dangerous territory by bringing up a fault in Quentin, I let it rip. "You know, it's customary for the Creative Director of an agency to hire his own copy chief, for chrissake."

There's a long pause in the conversation, during which time I picture being served my walking papers, and then, unexpectedly: "You're right, Bob. And I can see why you are pissed off with me for not having taken care of this."

Quentin looks suitably repentant. "I didn't want Ridgeley

jumping the gun and hiring some Boston hack," he says, "so I took the matter into my own hands and got you in instead. I had the perfect excuse if Ridgeley was to balk--that he was away working and that we needed a copy chief pronto because the previous one had, uh, died. I then left it with Powell to tell Ridgeley that you had been hired. He obviously didn't do it. All I can do is tell you how sorry I am."

Here's one of the most powerful people in the ad business, not to mention in the business world in general, apologizing to a mere regional copy chief. He didn't have to.

But I can't leave well enough alone. I have to, as usual, drive a point home till it's protruding from someone's skull. Without fully intending it and not being able to control my mouth, and risking everything, I go way out on a limb and don't seem to give a shit how Quentin takes it.

"Cut the crap, John. If this is the way you guys operate, I don't want any part of it. I think it's one of the shittiest tricks I ever heard of being played on somebody. I don't especially like the bastard, but he's a human being, a fact that you and Powell seem to have ignored."

Quentin is absolutely quiet, and then he says, "Listen, Bob, what you just said is exactly the reason I hired you. You won't take any garbage from anyone. Including me. I need people like you around me, people with integrity, people who won't yes me to death, and people to keep me in line. That's what I don't get from any of the staff here. You could hand me your resignation and I wouldn't accept it."

What Quentin doesn't understand is that what I just did wasn't an act of integrity. It was an act of professional suicide, an attempt to screw up my one chance in Boston, and one so warped that even Sigmund Freud would have trouble figuring it out.

That Quentin didn't take the bait, however, makes me breathe a sigh of relief in my head. He turns on the charm, the baby blues, the toothy smile, the whole package. The truth is, I don't want to lose this job. If my tantrum just now had worked,

I would have been devastated.

"I sincerely hope you know how much I regret the way we fucked up with Ridgeley and how you were put on the spot," Quentin says. "And I sincerely hope you will put this 'Ridgeley thing' behind you and that you will take my word for it that such a thing will never happen again."

Quentin now stands and walks over to me. "I'm appealing to you, Bob, because the last thing I want is for something like this to come between us."

I find what he has just said a little too intimate for my taste. It's his seductive style when dealing with either sex. But when you think about it, how many great generals have inspired their troops with such humbling statements? And how many young men were then willing to rush into battle to eagerly, even happily, give their lives with their leader's words ringing louder in their ears than the artillery exploding all around them?

I remember those documentaries of General Dwight D. Eisenhower, Supreme Commander of the Allied Forces in Europe during WWII, giving his troops a pep talk just before the D-Day landings. Those young guys, many of them soon to be dead, all stood there with complete faith in their leader. General Ike had amazing charisma.

So does General Quentin.

-32-

The "Ridgeley thing" may be settled between Quentin and me as far as Quentin is concerned, but it's hardly settled between Ridgeley and me.

He's bitchier than ever, throwing things against walls, screaming at people, refusing to give the green light on any ads I've approved. I try to stay out of his way, which is impossible right now because he's called a brainstorming session with the entire creative department.

We're all crammed into the conference room at the end of the workday. None of us wants to be here. We're tired, grumpy, hungry, and wanting to go home. These brainstorming sessions, usually brought about by panic, rarely produce anything other than more panic.

Little do I know at this point that there are some big surprises in store for all of us this very evening.

Ever since I started working here, the copywriters and art directors have maintained a wall between themselves and me. They've made it clear they *have* to work for me, but they are not required to *like* working for me.

The message they convey is that I'm a totally meaningless entity in their lives, put here by the New York office, earning a lot more money than they--and weird as well, judging from all the publicity I received after the fiasco at my last agency.

This cold front may or may not thaw. I will, obviously, have to earn their respect, a common occurrence in business, even if the person earning the respect is the boss.

Meanwhile, I have been sizing them up, too, ranking them in terms of strength and talent. The most valuable person in the creative department, and the agency, in general, and in the Boston advertising community for that matter, is the art director, Nelson Tanner, a dead ringer for Elvis Presley in a pudgy, extremely- dissipated kind of way; someone who is continually stoned out of his mind.

Nelson is the only one in the agency who understands this new thing called "hi-tech," and is therefore the only one qualified to handle our computer account and our five other hi-tech accounts. I, for one, can't make head or tail of them.

Those highly-lucrative accounts are strictly with AAB/Boston because of Nelson Tanner.

Any agency in town handling hi-tech products would love to have him on their staff, drugs and all, because he knows more on the subject than anyone, including some of the manufacturers. He's a hi-tech-knowledgeable superstar who looks and acts like a rock superstar. His wild, dyed-blonde hair cascades down his back and his outlandish clothes make him look like a pirate.

Those from the *fuck the consumer* school of advertising, Knas, Ferncliff, Santoro and Phipps are, without question, the least valuable.

Ferncliff has been especially vocal about this new regime and has let it be known he doesn't *like* the "direction" the agency is going in. In other words, he objects to me and everything I stand for. He has also let it be known that he is looking for another job. I hope that's true and also true of the other three. Their arrogance would be tolerable if they weren't so blatantly, dismally, and excruciatingly talentless.

The reason for the brainstorming session is that the Biggah Frozen Foods client has, just this afternoon, seen the final edit on the spots Ridgeley shot in L.A., and has threatened to fire the agency, burn the film and blow up our new projection room unless the commercials are rewritten, re-shot, and rescheduled immediately. At agency expense.

Ridgeley informs us that Hobart Powell expects new scripts

first thing in the morning—even if it takes all night to come up with them. Implicit in Ridgeley's message is that the writers and art directors are expected to work through the night. Or else.

Ridgeley, (along with *his* team of Knas, Ferncliff, Santoro and Phipps), is largely responsible for the doomed campaign which revolves around singing shrimp and dancing cod fillets. Right now, he is attempting to take the spotlight off himself for having done this terrible work, and transfer it to me.

"Aren't we lucky," he says, wearing his signature sneer, "to have in our presence a Clio Award-winning writer, hired by AAB's very own John Quentin in New York, to show us poor yokels in Boston how brilliant advertising is done. We are sooooooo fortunate to have him help us inferior creative types." I say nothing and just let him mouth off.

"Illuminate us, Bob, by telling us how you would get this project started, since you are obviously our genius creative guru." Ridgeley's tone is crawling with condescension.

His approach has worked. I'm now on the spot, not him. This is where I'm supposed to say something incredibly ingenious that he can immediately shoot down. The creative people have now deigned to look in my direction, but with cold eyes as they wait for me to crash and burn.

What I say is unexpected, even by myself. "Well, since you ask, I would start by going home, having a nice hot shower, dinner, some relaxation in front of the TV, and then eight hours sleep."

There is a "*Huh?*" on everyone's face. "And I would advise everyone else to do the same thing. Then, tomorrow, when we're rested and alert, we can get to work on this."

Ridgeley is, for once, speechless. He has fallen off his high horse, momentarily shaken out of his arrogant posturing. "Have you gone stark, raving mad?" he hisses, "Powell wants those scripts in the morning!"

"We all want things, Guy," I reply. "But that doesn't mean we can always have them."

There is complete silence in the room for a few seconds and

then somebody says: "Hey, everybody, we finally have someone with balls!" It's our producer, Nikki Wasserman.

"Now just one goddamn minute," Ridgeley says, reacting to Nikki's statement. "I happen to be the goddamned creative director of this goddamn agency. I can goddamn fire all of you if I wish. You think that what I am saying I am saying in jest? Well, anyone who dares leave this agency tonight can forget about having a job tomorrow."

"Yeah, yeah, yeah," Nelson Tanner says, yawning in Ridgeley's face.

Ridgeley is stunned. "You're fired," he yells. Nelson just laughs and the next thing I know, Ridgeley has whirled around and is pointing a bony finger in my face. "You," he says menacingly, "you are responsible for this. You think you New York hotshots can march into this agency and start a mutiny, create complete mayhem, turn the creative people against me."

"Guy," Rick says calmly, "face it. The creative people were against you long before Bob got here."

Ridgeley's humiliation is complete, and isn't what I intended. I feel sorry for him, but can't help him. In the ad biz, the act of reaching out to someone is dangerous, even suicidal. It's regarded as a sign of weakness, even by the person you are reaching out to.

"Very well," Ridgeley says dramatically while directing even more venom toward me, "*you* go to Powell tomorrow morning and *you* tell him yourself how you defied a direct order to have new scripts for him, Mr. Big Time Clio-Award Winner. Quentin may have all the creative power in this agency, but Hobart has the executive power. You cross him on this kind of issue and you are out!"

I'm taken unawares by what I hear next. "Hey Bob, would you like some company when you go see the old man tomorrow?" It's Healy Derekson, one of the two good writers. Nelson Tanner immediately follows Healy and offers to accompany me, as well. In the next minute, Nikki and Rick join in.

Am I hearing right? I have gone from leper to leader in less than twenty minutes? Not surprisingly, there's hardly a peep out Santoro, Ferncliff, Knas, or Phipps, the four deadheads.

There's nothing from Julie Ash, either. But for someone who hasn't given me a second glance since I've been with the agency, it now appears she can't take her eyes off me. It may be she doesn't believe in sticking her neck out, and who can blame her, but it's quite apparent I've made an impression on her, and it looks like quite a big one.

I'm grateful for those wanting to support me with Powell, only I can't accept their offers. "Thanks, but no thanks. Maybe you've heard? I have a knack at getting people fired."

It occurs to me that Santoro, Ferncliff, Knas and Phipps may stay all night with Ridgeley and come up with something to show Powell in the morning. Well, they can try, but it was their work that landed the agency in trouble in the first place.

-33-

My house, when I get home, is dark, dank and unfriendly. It needs a good cleaning lady, maybe even a live-in housekeeper, someone to cook the meals, do the washing. Like Allie used to do.

Did I regard Allie, before she left me, as a live-in housekeeper? She didn't usually get looped until evening. Daytimes were for taking really good care of the kids, cooking delicious meals, and keeping the house spotless.

Like a lot of alcoholics, she was a perfectionist who would have liked a perfect husband who went to work for the same company year after year, climbed the corporate ladder, and would one day receive a gold watch. I had enormous potential when starting out, leaving J.C. Penney and landing a job as a cub copywriter at a small agency called Smith/Greenland on Lexington and Fifty-eighth. It may have been small, but the work it turned out was revolutionary.

I was immediately in my element, coming up with ads that astonished even me. They were good, sometimes great. I'd no idea I had a talent for creating memorable ads, one after the other.

And then something even more fortuitous happened. When I was with Smith/Greenland about a year, Jerry Della Femina, creative director of another small shop, the legendary Delehanty, Kurnit and Geller, called me. He wanted to hire me and offered me two thousand dollars *over* my asking price. I had more than doubled my salary.

It was time to propose to Allie. Elated after this offer, and feeling the world my oyster, I headed straight for J.C. Penney where Allie, now head of women's sportswear, her brainchild, was in a meeting with her buyers and designers, all men. And I was going to crash it.

"You can't go in there," a secretary admonished me.

"No?" I'd said, "Just watch me."

Flinging open the doors to the boardroom, I entered, interrupting the proceedings.

"I've doubled my salary," I shouted. "Now we can get married!"

"Is that a proposal?" Allie had asked.

"You bet it is!"

Allie, head of the department as she was, rose from her chair and said: "Gentlemen, the meeting is adjoined."

We were totally in love, or so I thought, and were planning our wedding. But it wasn't as simple as that. On Allie's birthday, I had tickets for a Broadway show and was planning to take her to a really good restaurant for dinner. Only she stood me up. Without warning, she had flown to Arizona with a former boyfriend, Ned somebody, on his private jet.

Needless to say, I was devastated. Maybe she was hoping this other guy was going to marry her, give her a life of extreme financial privilege. But then he obviously didn't propose and suddenly, I was back in fashion. Maybe I should have let her go at this point. It might have been better for both of us. But I didn't let her go because I couldn't picture going through life without her.

Two weeks later, we eloped. Allie was then and is now, the love of my life.

Back home, taking off my jacket, I enter the kitchen, which is in a direct angle with Miss Martin's living room. If she cranes her neck, she can see me cooking my supper, ravioli out of a can. The preservative has the same odor I remember when I would open a can of dog food for a pet I once had. I stand there stirring the stuff, knowing Miss Martin is watching me.

Flicking off the overhead lights, I sit in our little breakfast nook, hidden from Miss Martin's view, depriving her of any more of my company. And then I fall asleep in the living room.

Much later, maybe even hours later, I get up and turn on the lights thinking Miss Martin must be in bed by now, probably disappointed I've been so anti-social this evening. After all, what else does this long-in-the-tooth, retired librarian and dedicated voyeur have to look forward to, but some sneak peeks in the neighbor's windows?

This ritual goes on every evening and I usually don't mind. At least I know someone is watching over me.

It must be close to midnight and I'm just about to go up to bed when someone leans on the front doorbell.

"Dammit" I say, thinking it must be Miss Martin. Who else could it be? Maybe she's sick. Maybe she wants me to take her to the hospital. She told me recently she wasn't feeling too well these days. I go to the door fully prepared to save Miss Martin's life, only it's not Miss Martin.

"I was just driving by," Julie Ash says. "Thought I'd drop in."

I've had virtually no conversation with her since I became copy chief. And here she is standing on my veranda. What is she doing here?

"I was just getting ready for bed," I tell her.

"Mind if I join you?"

-34-

Okay, that was crazy. What in the bloody hell was I doing? I don't know if Bertram is practicing anymore, but if not, maybe I should get someone else to examine my head. All I want is for Allie to come home and there I go acting like a complete idiot with Julie Ash.

Having said that, last night was fantastic. But it can't happen again. Aside from anything else, it's not a good idea sleeping with someone who works for you.

Anyway, it's the morning after and I'm in the office and I know there will probably be hell to pay for my actions during Ridgeley's brainstorming session last night. Powell, upon hearing of my refusal to work overnight will try to use this opportunity to get me canned.

My question is whether or not Quentin will agree with my views and try to keep me from getting canned. Will he *want* to keep me from getting canned? He may be mad as hell that I didn't stay all night to come up with a new campaign. It's the kind of thing they do in the New York agency; another reason the work there is so bad.

My first inquisitor of the day is Tod. "Am I to believe," he asks, "that what Ferncliff and Basker are telling me is true? That you flagrantly challenged Ridgeley's authority last night and that you totally thwarted his order to create a new campaign for Biggah, and told the writers to go home?"

"It's all true."

"So you weren't content in losing that account single-handedly at your last agency—you want to repeat your reckless behavior and lose us a major client here?"

"To the contrary," I say, "I think you've done a pretty good job losing this client all by yourself by approving those god-awful scripts Ridgeley came up with and shot in LA."

"Those scripts were greatly misunderstood."

"Oh sure, talking cows, singing chickens. You're right, they were too intellectual for the general public."

"Ridicule those commercials all you want, but what am I to tell my client who is scheduled to arrive at the agency at two-thirty this afternoon, and is expecting to see the new campaign?"

"Tell him to go away and come back in two weeks."

"Come back in two weeks? Come back in two weeks?"

"When we have something to show him."

"When we have something to show him? And when, dare I ask, when is that supposed to be?"

"Like I said, two weeks."

"I suggest you revise that to two hours," Tod says. "Otherwise neither Jesus nor your protector down in New York will be able to get you out of this mess."

"I don't know about Jesus," I say, 'but my protector, as you call him, has put me in this job to make sure the work isn't the same old garbage you guys have been turning out year after year." As I say this, I remember the same old garbage they turn out in New York, but never mind.

"That 'same old garbage' as you call it has made us one of the most profitable agencies in the AAB Group."

"That's not what I've heard. Before I got here, the folks down in New York were concerned that AAB/Boston was losing clients left and right to Boston's boutique agencies."

"Those agencies won't last long," Tod says mockingly, "and neither will you after your utterly stupid act last night. It may surprise you to know that even Quentin can't supersede the wishes of an important client. Headquarters allows Quentin complete say over the creative product, but he can't get in the way of Client/Agency relations. In this office, you have to deal with Hobart Powell on that issue."

Tod has a point. A major point. The same one Ridgeley made last night. And one that definitely affects me and the decision I made when I told everyone to go home.

Getting the work to the client on time is Powell's domain. He can build a case against me that even Quentin may not be able to defend. That's assuming, again, that Quentin would *want* to defend such an action. I haven't heard from him today, so who knows?

"By the way, Tod," I say, "why are you coming to me? Why aren't you complaining to Ridgeley? He's the creative director, you know."

Exasperated and almost unable to speak, Tod glares at me. "Ridgeley isn't in yet. He hasn't called in. Nobody knows where he is." He says this as if that's my fault, too. He then stomps off, yellow Brooks Brothers button-down shirt, red suspenders and flapping blue, orange and green plaid tie, an example of the usual tasteless attire worn by account executives in their misled attempt to look hip.

A little while later Rick, Healy, Nelson and Nikki come to see me, ostensibly to show me a TV concept, but really because they're worried about me getting fired.

"You're the absolute best thing that's happened to this agency," Nikki says, "and we don't want to lose you."

"That's right," Rick says. "We all thought you were a total loser when we first saw you, but now we're not quite sure." A backhanded compliment.

-35-

Quick call to Bertram's office. I haven't seen him since this job began. I didn't have time. His receptionist tells me he's taken a leave of absence, and won't be back for the foreseeable future. Would I like an appointment with one of the other psychiatrists who share a practice with Dr. Perlberg?

So his dementia finally caught up with him. What do I do now? Maybe I should call John Quentin instead, but what if he says I screwed up? I call anyway and am told by his secretary that he's in Europe at a big AAB summit meeting over there. No wonder he hasn't called. Does he even know about my refusal to work or have my writers work last night?

I get up from my desk, and like a zombie, walk to the door. Even though Powell hasn't called me to his office, I may as well get the confrontation over and done with.

Stacks of papers sit on my desk. There are requisitions for new ads and current ads to be copy-proofed. There are layouts to be approved and briefs for new assignments. There's so much work to be done it's mind boggling—and I'm the engine pushing it.

We're short-handed, which means every staff member has to triple his or her workload. I was planning to call Bunny about getting a couple of additional copywriters and art directors. I may not have to make that call once I see Powell.

Opening my office door, I cautiously peer out. My secretary, Sondra, is at her desk. She looks up at me and smiles sympathetically. She knows what's going on. Everybody in the agency knows what's going on. If I'm reading Sondra right, she's probably wondering how long I'll be her boss.

Well, no matter what happens, I'm not going to make any apologies to Powell for my actions. The old bastard can rant and rave all he wants. If I'm going to lose this job, I'm going to lose it on my terms.

Still, I hope there won't be major repercussions. I'm always standing up for something and have considered that I may have some sort of martyr complex. This is the pattern Bertram was always talking about. Dammit, Bertram, why did you have to lose your mind when I most needed you?

An image of the famous New York copywriter, Helen Nolan, suddenly pops up in my mind's eye as I walk down the hall. Helen, a raven-haired woman of immense talent and power, was a group head in the second agency I worked in. I remember her remark when I'd made a big fuss over something or other in a meeting with a client.

Helen said after the meeting: "You should never open your big, Jewish mouth. Never open it for anything. Eat all your meals intravenously." Excellent advice I've never forgotten. Or, for that matter, used.

I'm just getting ready to duke it out with Powell when, as I approach his office, I hear a series of loud female shrieks. They get louder and louder as I get closer. Marie, sitting at her desk, is sobbing her heart out. What's the matter? What's happened? It's shocking to see this.

Another secretary is soothingly trying to console Marie. I ask her what's wrong.

"It's Mr. Powell," she whispers. "He's been in an automobile accident."

I say the first thing that pops into my head and it comes out sounding like I'm elated. "Is he dead?"

Marie, who has heard me, screams: "Yes, he's dead, crushed to death like a bug," she says in one, long howl. "Some dirty, sneaking, bastard murdered him!"

The concerned secretary takes me aside. "Marie just got a

call from Mr. Powell's son. Apparently, Mr. Powell was walking to his car after a visit to his club last night, when another driver came along, crossed over the center dividing line and struck Mr. him. He suffered major trauma to the body--a crushed pelvis and terrible leg wounds. The driver of the other car then backed up and struck again, crushing Mr. Powell's head and chest."

This is unbelievable. "Did they catch the driver?" I ask.

"No," she says. "There was only one witness, some distance away, who couldn't make out the license plate or make of the car, but said it crossed over to where Mr. Powell was and deliberately hit him."

Marie is still crying. She's older than the other secretaries, probably twice their ages, and she has been with Powell for many years, a sort of office wife. She looks at me, her eyes narrowing, and in a low, spiteful hiss, says: "Where were you last night? Maybe it was you driving that car! Maybe it was you who killed Hobart!"

Her accusation hits me like a ton of bricks. What if somebody were to believe her? It's true that because Powell probably would have fired me today I might have taken care of him last night. It's plausible. And then there was the way I must have looked when hearing Powell was dead—like I wanted to order champagne for everyone.

Somehow or other, I just can't work up a mournful expression, even though I am shocked. I get back to my office as fast as possible and close the door.

-36-

No one else is mourning Powell's sudden departure, either. Instead, there's a sense of jubilation in the halls and offices, with people gathered around the water coolers, laughing animatedly. It's like a national holiday, only better.

But nothing in an ad agency stays the focus of conversation for long. Not even the sensational news of the managing director having been murdered, or the speculation as to who did it or who will take his place as general manager.

It would seem that Tod would be the logical choice for general manager in which case I may as well pack up and get out, but agency gossip has it that Tod isn't aggressive enough getting new clients. Because of this, New York is probably waiting to see how he does as an interim general manager and with new acquisitions proposals. Interim is okay. I can live with that.

More current is the topic that has replaced the mysterious death of Hobart Powell, and that's the mysterious disappearance of Guy Ridgeley. At first, it appeared he'd taken a day off, but then we discovered that he was gone, as in "gone forever."

He must have removed his personal stuff--pictures, books, and files after the brainstorming session last night, when it was apparent to all, including himself, that he had completely lost control of the creative department. Additionally, there's a hastily-scribbled note from Ridgeley left on his desk telling AAB/Boston to go fuck itself.

I am, of course, wondering what's up next, and who was Powell's executioner? For most of the staff, the lore of that person, still at large, has elevated him to hero status. I could swear some of the employees are regarding me with especial respect—they must really think that I'm the murderer. After all, a man who would actually destroy a Chagall probably wouldn't think twice about killing someone.

They're not the only ones who have this idea. I've been considered a possible suspect by the police as well, thanks to Powell's secretary, Marie, broadcasting it all over the agency that I was the culprit. According to this madwoman, I had good reason to kill Powell in that there was going to be a showdown and I was about to be fired.

When questioned by a team of detectives who've come to the agency, I explain that I was home at the time of Powell's appointment with an assassin. Their reply is, "Got a witness?"

"Well, no, I live alone," I tell them. I don't want to implicate Julie. In fact, I don't want it getting out that she was there at all. What if Allie were to hear about it? Just at the point when I think these goons are going to handcuff me and take me down to the police station, I have a flash of genius. I have a second witness. A very observant one.

Later on, after Miss Martin has corroborated my alibi, saying that I got home at exactly 9:25 in the evening, and was home during the time Powell was pinned against his car, I'm off the hook. She even reported that it was 11:56 p.m. when I went up to bed.

Good old Miss Martin. She hadn't mentioned Julie's late arrival, a fact that she was of course, well aware of.

Good old John Quentin, too. Because immediately upon his return from Europe and hearing of Powell's death and Ridgeley's departure, he makes me the new creative director of AAB/ Boston.

"It's all yours, kid," he says on the phone. "The whole creative operation of Abbott, Ayler, Ballard/Boston. It's your new franchise. Go for it! Make it into the best goddamn franchise on the planet!"

-37-

Here it is, less than two months since I joined the agency and all of a sudden, I'm the creative director of AAB/Boston. How I went so rapidly from being totally unemployable to being in the most-prestigious creative position of anyone in Boston's advertising world is scaring me to death.

It's an effort to keep my self-destructive side under control. What can I do to screw it all up?

Fortunately, there isn't anything at the moment that would make me throw a fit or create a catastrophe for myself. No clients demanding asinine changes to our concepts or copy, no more Ridgeley and his poisonous personality, and at the moment, no problems with the account execs other than for Tod, who seethes hatred every time he sees me.

I do have a problem with an overworked staff, however. We desperately need more people. I call Bunny Berger's archrival, Sylvia Lowenbach, to engage her in finding me some really good art directors and writers willing to transfer from New York to Boston--although I am wondering why a really good A.D. or writer would want to come to a backwater like Boston.

The first person Sylvia sends me is a New York art director by the name of Carl Mayler. But when he arrives for his interview, two people and a dog enter my office. One is a stocky, dark-haired young man and the other is a short, dumpy brunette carrying a poodle.

"I hope you don't mind I brought my wife, Sheila," Carl says, shaking my hand. "She was afraid to be left alone in the car."

"No," I say, as if it's absolutely normal having the wife there. "How are you?" I ask Carl.

"Exhausted," Sheila answers for him. "We drove from Brooklyn. Took forever. I just hope this trip is worth it."

I turn to Carl who looks like he'd like to clamp a palm over Sheila's mouth.

Cutting to the chase, I ask to see Carl's work. It's excellent. He has mainstream ad experience and hi-tech experience as well. The latter is an extra plus in case Nelson gets into deep water with his drug use or with the law, due to his habit of protesting everything from the Vietnam War to the cruel usage of animals in research.

"I like your work," I say.

"You'd have to be an asshole not to," Sheila says.

"Sheila, watch your language, will you? I'm on an interview here."

"Sorry," Sheila says. "Say, how much does this job pay, anyway?"

"Sheila!" Carl hisses.

"No, it's all right for Sheila to ask," I say. "How much do you want?"

I've directed the question to Carl, but Sheila answers.

"Oh, I don't know," Sheila says. "About seventeen five?"

"Sheila," Carl says, "Mr. Bronson is addressing me, not you, okay? Now either hold your tongue or, hold your tongue."

"I think I'll go piddle," Sheila says. "Where's the terlit?"

"Down the hall," I say. "My secretary will show you the way."

"I'm really sorry about this, Mr. Bronson," Carl says when Sheila has gone. "I should have left Sheila in the reception area, or better than that, in New York."

"Don't worry about it, Carl." I say, and am about to offer him the job when Nikki walks in.

"Say, who's the weirdo with the dog I saw in the reception area?" she asks.

"After a long moment of awkward silence, "That's my wife," Carl says.

"Oops," Nikki says.

"Carl, meet Nikki, one of our TV producers."

Nikki spies some of Carl's ads on my desk and grabs a handful. "Wow, Bob, hire this guy immediately."

"I was just about to do just that when you interrupted," I say tersely. "Is there something I can help you with, Nikki?"

"No, I just want to remind you we have the radio commercials for Benton's Carpets to take care of in the morning."

I already know the client has approved the whole lot and said he especially liked the one with the opening: "Hi, I'm Bud Williams and I'm six feet two, but when I stand on a Benton's lush, luxurious, deep pile carpeting, I'm five feet eleven...."

"So what do you think?" I ask Carl after Nikki has left. "Do you want the job?"

"If Sheila is willing to leave her mother, I'm willing."

As if on cue, there's a knock on the door. It's Sheila.

"Hi, it's the exile back from Shark Island. So what have you two decided?"

"We've decided that if you're willing to move up here, I'm willing, too," Carl says.

"Willing—of course, I'm willing. Why wouldn't I be willing?"

"Carl was afraid you'd miss your mother," I say.

"Miss my mother? You gotta be joking. It was Carl who cried the first night he was away from his mother, which happened to be our wedding night." Sheila answers.

"I think we'd better be going, Sheila," Carl says between clenched teeth. "Mr. Bronson is busy."

"Let's go then," Sheila says. "Who's keeping you here? Come, Daphne," she says to the dog.

"When can you start?" I ask, walking them to the door.

"Two weeks unless you need me sooner," Carl says.

"You are paying our moving expenses, I assume?" Sheila asks.

"I'll have to check," I say. "I'm not sure of the agency pol-"

"Because if they're not paid, maybe Carl won't be able to accept the job after all, you know what I mean?" Sheila's like the

Jewish Mafia.

"I think something can be arranged," I say quickly.

"Well, I'm very happy that I'll be working with you," Carl says, and then turns to his wife with a wait-until-I-get-you-outside look on his face.

"Same here," I say. "And if you have any problems, just let me know."

"Don't worry," Sheila says. "We will."

-38-

"You got Carl Mayler from Sylvia Lowenbach??" Bunny Berger screams into the phone, practically causing me permanent hearing loss.

Her eyes are everywhere. Had she been employed by military intelligence during WWII, development of the Enigma ciphering decoder wouldn't have been necessary.

I know Bunny could get revenge on me for going to Sylvia instead of her. To her way of thinking, this would be defined as a capital crime. And should I ever be out of a job again, she could make it impossible for me to get in anywhere.

"Where's the gratitude?" she asks. "Where's the loyalty? I get you situated in a great job with John Quentin when nobody else will touch you with a ten-foot pole and you go to Sylvia Lowenbach? Well, okay if that's the way you want to play it, just don't come to me when they fire you. And I wouldn't be surprised if that happens next week, with your job record."

I say nothing because I know this rampage of Bunny's is leading somewhere. And I'm right.

"Of course," she says, suddenly sort of kittenish, "you could redeem yourself. You need a new copy chief and I have the perfect candidate for you, someone you already know, someone who worships the ground you walk on."

"Can't think of anyone by that description, Bunny," I say.

"Not even Lorne Chambers?"

Lorne? Is she kidding?

"I don't get it, Bunny. He's got a job. He's the creative director of Masters, Jepson, Pollack, Vincent and Sharone."

"You mean he *was* the creative director of Masters, Jepson, Pollack, Vincent and Sharone. He's been replaced."

"Replaced?" I exclaim. "I thought he had the place sewn up."

"That's what he thought. Until they told him he was out. It appears he couldn't get the creative product together. Anyway, being canned, he thought you would be happy to employ him, seeing as you and he are such good friends. And how you need a copy chief."

"Wait a minute, Bunny. He couldn't get the creative product together at Masters, Jepson, and you want me to hire him as my copy chief?"

Lorne, who never once gave me the time of day when I was out of work now expects me to come through for him. Boy, does he have balls.

"No matter what happened at that agency, he's got a terrific book," Bunny says.

"Don't I know it," I say, remembering most of the work in his book came from my brain.

"And he really likes you. Admires you, in fact. He really does. He told me that if it hadn't been for your help, he might never have made it in advertising."

"That's an understatement," I say, positive in my mind that no matter what this flesh-eating spider says to warm me up or wear me down, I will not see Lorne. Not if he writes, phones, pleads or begs.

"So can I at least tell him you'll see him?' Bunny probes. "At least that much?

"No, Bunny, you cannot tell him that."

"Well, I can't force you to have compassion for a dear old friend," Bunny says. "By the way, after they fired Lorne, it just so happened that I had exactly the right man to replace him with."

"I'm sure you did, Bunny, I'm sure you did," I think to myself.

"Ever hear of Guy Ridgeley, former Creative Director of Abbott, Ayler Ballard/Boston? Don't go looking for Santini, Ferncliffe, Knas or Phipps, either. He took them with him."

The four deadheads. Come to think of it, I hadn't seen them around this past week. I'd been giving them nothing but inferior assignments in the hope that they would quit. This has turned out better than I imagined and I didn't have to do a thing. They walked out on their own, no notice or anything. I'm grateful to Bunny.

But not so grateful that I'm willing to see Lorne Chambers. That will never happen, absolutely never.

-39-

That being the case, what am I doing having lunch with him in an Italian restaurant on Newberry Street a week later?

"Wouldn't it be great if we could work together?" he is saying.

"Nope," I answer. We've eaten and I just sit there listening to Lorne rattle on and on.

"Why not? Because I didn't phone you for a couple of months? What's a couple of months between friends?"

Neither one of us has asked the waiter for the bill. That's because neither one of us intends to pay it. As usual, I would have picked it up, but I'm not inclined to give Lorne a thing.

"Oh, can it, will you, Lorne? I'm sick of that line of crap you hand out." Actually, I'm rather enjoying being in a position where he's come begging. He's one of the most selfish and devious characters I have ever known. And one of the phoniest.

"What line? What crap? I was worried about you every day when you were out of work. You can ask Dina if I wasn't worried."

"You were so worried, you couldn't call me to see if I was still alive?"

"Oh, now you're being dramatic. Still alive!"

I let it pass. This is classic Lorne—completely unconscious and full of shit.

"How's Allie, by the way?"

"She left me," I say, dully.

"No," Lorne says.

"Yes."

"Gone to live with her sister, huh?"

"How did you know?"

"I just guessed it." Lorne says, lying as usual. He is sure to have heard the news through his wife, Dina, who is a friend of Margaret Bloch who is a friend of Sarah Wallingford who is a friend of Bellissa Fishman who is a friend of Ginger Scooby who will have heard it from Denise Lawson.

"Well, what about it?" Lorne asks.

"What about what?"

"What about a job? Come on, you know there's a job up there for me."

"I don't know, Lorne. I don't think AAB is the best place for you."

"Why not?" Lorne asks.

"Because you would be campaigning to get my job in no time."

"You must be crazy. We've been friends for years. You helped me get where I am today."

"Out on the street?'

"Don't be funny," Lorne says. "That's only temporary since I quit my job."

"You were fired."

"It was mutual."

"It was one-sided. Them against you."

"It wasn't that way."

"Everybody in that agency—in fact everybody in Boston— knows about it. Most people in Boston hate your guts. They consider you a slimy, ego-maddened shit."

"That's ridiculous," Lorne says. "I'm a sweet person. Look at me, don't I look like a sweet person?"

I look at Lorne wondering how we could have been friends for so many years, since our days at Straubenmuller Textile High School on West 18th street in Manhattan where he always stole my girl and wore my new jackets and sweaters before I did.

He even tried to get Allie in the sack between our engagement and marriage. Forgive me, Allie, for not believing you then about that, but I do now.

Thinking about it, I get so angry, I slap Lorne across the head.

"Hey," Lorne says, warding off any more blows, "why'd you do that? Are you nuts or something?"

"That's for attacking Allie."

"Attacking Allie? What the hell are you talking about?"

"It was before Allie and I were married and you tried to rape her."

"You know there are effective treatments for people with your emotional problems," Lorne says, taking a little mirror from his breast pocket and surveying the damage my slap might have done to his carefully coifed hair.

I watch him for a moment or two as he is completely engrossed by his image, and then I can't stand it any longer. I motion to the waiter. There's a look of triumph on Lorne's face that I'm picking up the tab again.

"Give it to him," I tell the waiter.

"Jesus, man, I'm out of work," Lorne complains.

"My heart bleeds for you, Lorne, but you asked me out to lunch, remember?"

"Bastard," Lorne says, laughing. "You really are something, you know? I think those couple of months I didn't speak to you really helped you out. You're more of a man. Not such a pussy. You have more confidence, more chutzpah. I think I like the new Bob Bronson."

"Just pay the damn bill," I say.

We walk out of the restaurant and along Newberry Street.

"So you gonna bail me out, kid?" Lorne asks. "It's a long, long winter in Boston and I don't want to be caught in the middle of it without a job."

I think about all the times I have rescued Lorne. I'd been doing that all my life. But I'll be damned if I'm going to do it this time. Hell will freeze over first. I mean it.

It isn't even a week after I've had lunch with Lorne that I hire him.

-40-

Who am I kidding? I knew all along that I was going to hire him. I knew it the minute Bunny first mentioned him being out of a job. I knew it before we got together for lunch.

I have always been powerless over Lorne Chambers. It's been that way ever since we were teenagers when he was the only kid who didn't say I was weird. He was my friend. My only friend. He would bolster my spirits all those times when I was depressed--which was *all* the time.

But there was a reason he went to all that trouble, and it had nothing to do with him being a friend. It took a very long time, but it finally did occur to me just why he was so solicitous. Lorne's strict mother would never let him go out at night, but she liked me and thought I was a good influence, so she let him go to the movies with me.

Not that we ever actually went to the movies. As soon as I sprang Lorne from his house, he was gone. Right away he would take off without me for the local poolroom where he liked to hang out with his friends. I was the patsy and let this happen dozens of times.

And now, this very same Lorne Chambers is whining. "You expect me to process those?" He's referring to the pile of requisitions on his desk waiting for him. "I'm going to need an assistant."

"No assistant," I tell him. "I was able to get through the copy chief workload and be the creative director at the same time."

"Well, we're not all hyper," is Lorne's reply. "I'll get to the job orders right after lunch."

He says this at half past-ten in the morning.

"You'll get to them right now." I say.

"Okay, boss, don't have a conniption fit," Lorne says and goes into his office, ostensibly to work. But half an hour later, Al Marino, the traffic guy, comes crashing into my office complaining that nothing has been done on the reqs and that no one can locate Lorne.

The whole thing is maddening and I can't do anything about it right now because Quentin has me going to Puerto Rico to shoot a commercial and Sondra is telling me I have to leave right this minute if I'm going to catch the plane on time. I grab my suitcase and go.

The product we're filming is Puerto Rican rum. The rum may be of a high quality, but the script is anything but. I don't know how Quentin could have passed it. Yes I do. He passes all that really awful New York stuff, doesn't he?

Arriving in San Juan, I find the situation a bit awkward because the New York creative team working on this project is down there as well and is extremely hostile to my intrusion. Even the film crew, hired out of Miami, looks put out.

I fully understand how I could get shoved down the hotel elevator shaft, especially when I unabashedly rewrite the script and quickly call Quentin to get it approved. Quentin loves it and tells me to "Go for it." I'm getting more and more suspicious when he says he loves something.

We're shooting on the beach at the famous Miramar Hotel resort. It's a world of the rich and famous, complete with the fancy cabanas and outdoor bar and waiters in tuxes taking drink orders at the pool and by the ocean.

The original script has a young couple, Jim and Tina, sitting around the pool drinking the rum. And that's it. Boring. In my rewrite, I introduce a third party I call Max. I don't have to look far for an actor to play Max because the hotel is full of American actors. Max is written into the script as a pal of Jim's who just so happens to be vacationing at the resort at the same time.

As the action begins, Jim and Max are at the outdoor bar when Jim mentions how he's just waiting for his girlfriend, Tina, to join him. He wants to buy Max a drink, but Max can't decide what to order.

"Why not try a Regents Rum on the rocks?" Jim suggests. "It's light, but full-bodied at the same time, and it's refreshing, too."

Just then, Tina appears. She's a bikini-clad knockout who rushes up to Jim, gives him a passionate kiss and asks him what he's having. But before he can answer, Max, instantly attracted to Tina and obviously planning to steal her away for himself, answers for Jim in a sexy tone: "Regents Rum, sweetheart. It's light, but full-bodied at the same time, and it's refreshing, too."

Tina is immediately swept off her feet by him. While she and Max are lost in a world of their own, the camera pans to Jim who has obviously lost his girlfriend. The spot ends with a close-up on his face as he realizes what happened.

The commercial is a wrap in two days and I'm back in Boston. There's still the problem with Lorne. Apparently he hasn't been around much and the job requisitions that were on his desk are still on his desk. Untouched.

Inviting Lorne into the agency is the same as inviting bubonic plague. And to give him the number two spot in the creative department? What insanity. I'd like to tell him the deal is off, but even with someone as useless as Lorne, I don't feel I can do that to him.

Without wanting to be, I'm still Lorne's caretaker. I suppose I always will be.

-41-

I may not have a reliable copy chief, but I have a group of extremely reliable and talented copywriters and art directors. And one thing I know about them is that they work for more than just a salary. They work for recognition. Every print ad, radio commercial and TV spot they produce is the result of intense creative effort.

Those ads become samples they can put in their portfolios and can be entered in awards functions. Winning an award is the vehicle that gets promotions and lucrative job offers.

There are other ways to get somewhere in the ad biz even for very talented people. One day during lunch hour when the agency is relatively quiet, Julie Ash comes to my office. I watch as she closes the door behind her and then locks it. Then she comes toward me and gets down on her knees at my feet.

Blow jobs are quite common in ad agencies. Secretaries are often promoted to junior writers or art directors as a reward.

This would definitely be a midday diversion, but I'm not interested. I wasn't faithful to Allie on a couple of occasions, the most recent time being a few weeks before with Julie, but from now on I will be, even if she and I are separated. In time, I might be able to get her back. I gently lift Julie to her feet.

"Don't you like me?" she asks.

"Julie, listen, what happened that night was a mistake. I'm a married man. Allie and I are just separated, not divorced. I love my wife and want her back."

"Well, she obviously doesn't love you or want you back. But

suit yourself," Julie says as she unlocks the door and leaves.

As it turns out, what she says about Allie not wanting me back is true. When I get home and check the mail, there's an important looking letter in the bunch. It's from a law firm in Boston. Inside is a petition that Allie has brought about for divorce.

Wait. I thought that Allie was considering coming back to me. I was counting on it. I really thought there was a chance for us. What happened? Then I get it...Beryl happened.

-42-

Ever since Allie left me, and I got this job and have felt support from John Quentin, I have more confidence. I don't even relate to the old Bob Bronson and his neurotic and irresponsible ways. The Bob Bronson who put his foot through the client's portrait is like some distant relative, no one I want to be around.

I really thought Allie could see the change in me, but apparently I was wrong. The best way to get through this is to keep busy. That's no problem. I'm busy as hell as is everyone in the creative department with the exception of Lorne.

And Nelson Banner.

I'm a bit apprehensive about Nelson because he keeps getting busted for his highly-vocal anti-war behavior that puts him right in the middle of the current political unrest. I don't want to lose Nelson. He could get locked up with the key thrown away. No one at AAB/Boston knows what he knows. Even on Route 128 with its string of technology companies, you'd be hard-pressed to find another Nelson.

It's because of his knowledge that he can get away with anything and everything in the agency. He can miss a deadline or show up at a client meeting high as a kite, or not show up at all. Our clients forgive him his faults because they know he holds the key to getting their products sought after, even if the work he does is on his terms and no one else's. His attitude is that he's just as phenomenal as the products he is putting on the map.

In his office, he likes to blast the rock stations on his radio so loud they can be heard (quite a distance away) in the reception area; or he'll play his electric guitar at an ear-shattering pitch.

If he makes mistakes in his work, no one in the agency and usually on the client side has the smarts to detect them, because no one other than Nelson has a clue, not even some of the people who've come up with this technology.

All this is well and good, but on a day-to-day basis, I can't be sure if Nelson will be on the job, or if he's been thrown in a jail or overdosed. You never know.

That goes double for Lorne Chambers.

-43-

The traffic guys are going crazy because there are, as usual, a couple of dozen new jobs that have to be assigned to writers and art directors, all with urgent due dates. Lorne hasn't made the slightest stab at getting this work done. In fact, he's hardly ever around. So when he does venture in one afternoon, I'm not exactly friendly.

"Nice of you to drop in," I say icily.

"Well, aren't *we* in a cheerful mood," Lorne replies.

"Look, Lorne," I say, "I've given you chance after chance and you don't seem to care if you keep this job or not."

"So what's your point?" Lorne asks. He looks genuinely puzzled.

"What's my point?" I ask, uncomprehendingly. "Well, I'll tell you what my point is. My point is that if you don't get your act together, you can beg all you want, and it won't save your ass."

This is when Lorne laughs in my face. "Nobody's told you?"

"Told me what?"

"I don't work for you anymore, buddy boy. I now work for Tod Lawson."

All the color in my face has probably drained out. I'm not sure, but I think I have to hold on to something. The pretense of friendship Lorne displayed in getting the job of copy chief is completely absent from his demeanor. In its place is a mocking sneer.

I just look at him, dumbfounded. A queasy sensation is rising in my gut. And, strangely, this feeling has nothing whatsoever to do with Lorne, but with me. This is my payoff for having sabotaged myself. For the last couple of months I have felt okay about myself, but now that old feeling of unworthiness has returned. It's what I am used to. It's what feels familiar. It's what I deserve.

"Did you really think I would take on all that work, Bobbie Boy?" Lorne says. "To really be a copy chief? The worst job in the world? Christ, I took one look at all those job orders sitting on my desk and said to myself, is that guy nuts?"

"So you went crying to Tod and he took you in?"

"Let's just say, he and I have major plans for the agency. That may or may not include you."

"I always knew you were a shit, Lorne, but I didn't know you were the whole cesspool."

"Yeah, well," Lorne says, ignoring my remark, "just thought I would stop by and let you know my new address."

I watch Lorne as he exits my office and realize I can't really blame him. I knew what I was doing when I brought him in. Things were going too well for me. I had to do something totally self-destructive. Lorne was the answer.

And I know he's going to be more trouble being out of the creative department than in.

LEANING ON THIN AIR

-44-

Almost instantly, I am right. Tod assigns Lorne to the Biggah campaign. So now I have him making a fuss over everything, including how long it is taking to get the work done. Rick and Healy have been working on it non-stop ever since the Ridgeley debacle without much success. It's very hard to get anything past me.

I've told Tod to keep Lorne out of the creative department, that he'll have to wait until we are good and ready to present. Requesting anything of Tod is, of course, futile. I should always remember that.

The research for Biggah indicates that ninety-eight percent of products in the frozen aisle are suffering from declining sales, and once kids grow up and leave home, quick-frozen dinners lose their appeal. Instead of eating frozen meals, the younger generation depends on what is being called "fast food" by the media. Franchises such as MacDonald's have sprung up around the country.

If we can persuade this younger generation that Biggah's frozen dinners are tastier than greasy luncheonette food, we might be able to get this segment of the market back. To remedy the downturn in Biggah's market share, we focus on worried, overprotective mothers who try to get their grown kids to eat better. With that in mind, Rick and Healy have come up with a concept with possibilities.

In a campaign of six commercials, we use the "mother theme" in a comical way. The first spot takes place at a wedding with the bride and groom opening their gifts. When the couple open the mother's gift, they are surprised to find, instead of a toaster or blender, a Biggah Gourmet Frozen dinner, and then another, and another. In the crowd, we see the mom looking satisfied.

A second spot features an astronaut in space who is suddenly surrounded by floating Biggah frozen dinners, courtesy of his mother. Still another shows a young college kid unpacking his suitcase in his dorm for the first time. It's packed with Biggah products, obviously slipped in by mom.

There are three other scripts based on the same theme, all with voiceover assurance that these meals are the best that a caring mother could wish for a beloved child. If executed properly, the product could snag more sales than any relaunch in a decade. Out of curiosity, I ask whose concept it was, Healy's or Rick's.

"Neither one of us," Healy says. "It was Julie's. She saw we were struggling and stepped in. We just helped a bit. She couldn't be here to present to you today."

"She didn't want to tell you, Bob, but she's pretty sick," Rick says. Sick? And she didn't want to tell me? What's wrong with her?"

"She's over at Mass General this morning getting tests done," Rick says. "According to Julie, the doctors say it could be leukemia."

-45-

Leukemia! Julie? How can that be? Looking at her, you would think she'd never been sick in her life. The news of her potentially fatal illness spreads fast and creates a shock wave not only in the creative department, but all over the agency. Funny how you might not think too much about a person until that someone falls ill.

I find myself very concerned about Julie--just like the others. Only in my case it's not just because I'm thinking of Julie in her hour of crisis, but because selfishly, I don't want to lose such a great talent. This callous attitude changes by late afternoon when I get a call from her. She's crying on the other end of the line and suddenly, I'm all mushy.

"I told Rick and Healy not to say anything and they told you anyway. Am I going to be fired? I don't want to be fired," she says between sobs. "I can still work. I love my work. I love the agency. I love working for you. I couldn't stand it if I couldn't work. You've been a wonderful boss and the time with you has been the best I've ever had in my life. Please don't fire me."

"Are you home?" I ask.

"Yes."

"I'll grab some of the others and we'll be right over."

"Just you," she says. "Don't bring anyone else. I just want you,"

-46-

I have to say, I didn't want it to happen, but my sympathy for Julie led to something other than a professional relationship. In the months to come, I'll look at this as a defining moment in my life, a moment I'll come to regret.

Allie is gone and maybe it's time for a new relationship. The only problem is that, if it's with Julie, I could be bringing in someone who might soon be dead. Everyone in the agency is rooting for her, telling her how great she looks, how she will be okay, how the test results, when they are *finally* back, will show this is all a false alarm.

Despite this extremely scary time, Julie exhibits extraordinary strength. Her courage is inspirational to behold. How can she pick up her work as if nothing has happened? Her bright demeanor has elevated her to heroine status. We're all in awe.

Then we find out that the doctors have told her that the test results show that she has chronic Leukemia which, is supposed to be marginally better than having acute leukemia because it doesn't spread as fast. But whichever kind, there's a very good chance it will take over and kill her. The question is when? How long does she have before it happens?

A few evenings after the bad news, we're at her apartment and Julie has a request. "Would you please close your eyes for a minute? I'll tell you when to open them." When I open them, I see she is completely bald and is holding a wig in her hands. It's a big jolt.

"They told me I would lose my hair," Julie says, trying to

laugh and failing, "so I beat them to it and got my head shaved. Do you mind sleeping with Yul Brynner?"

At this moment, I surrender my heart to her. She is so endearing, so vulnerable, so brave. You just want to hold her in your arms and do something to make all the bad stuff go away.

-47-

Work is Julie's best medicine. As soon as she, Rick and Healy put the finishing touches on the Biggah campaign, I arrange a trip down to New York to review the work with John Quentin. He will be the final arbiter. I would like to take Julie with me—can she make the trip?

"I may be sick, but I'm not dead," she quips.

A few days later, we're in Quentin's office. Julie looks fine with her wig neatly in place. She's highly professional as she presents the campaign with the aid of expertly drawn storyboards.

When she's done, Quentin actually applauds. He's warm and chummy, treating us like his two favorite people on earth. He certainly doesn't bestow such a friendly manner on the creative staff here in New York. In fact, it seems as if he actively dislikes them.

"If it was up to them," Quentin says, "I'd never go out to lunch. They even get mad when I go take a leak."

When Olga comes in to tell her boss the coast is clear and there's no one waiting for Quentin outside his door, she mentions that we have a lunch reservation at the Forum of the Twelve Caesars. The three of us escape, running for the elevator before someone sees us. We laugh like kids all the way to the ground floor. We exit the AAB/Worldwide Building, two pals and a much-liked gal on the loose, when an unshaven man wearing a shapeless overcoat and the worn-out shoes of a panhandler approaches us.

"John," the man says. For a moment, Quentin looks at him

and then a wave of recognition crosses his face.

"My God," Quentin exclaims, looking shocked.

"I've been waiting here," the man says, "waiting to see you."

"Hey Bob, Julie, walk on ahead," Quentin says. "I'll catch up with you in a minute." We walk to the corner of Fifty-fourth and Madison. I wonder what that's all about, but decide it's none of my business.

Quentin is standing there talking to the man and then he takes some money out of his wallet and presses it into the man's hand. The man drops the money on the sidewalk, not huffily, but patiently, as if the money has nothing to do with what he wants. Presently, Quentin walks off, leaving the man standing there and the money blowing up the street.

"Sorry about that," he says, catching up to us. "That used to be one of the best copywriters in the business. Maxwell Baker. He was my number two-man."

I had heard of Baker, and that he had worked with Quentin, a wunderkind who had suddenly disappeared.

"What happened to him?" I ask.

"Oh, the inevitable. You know...people go their own ways."

"He's sure a mess now," I say.

Quentin shoots me a funny look. "I suppose it's my fault," he says.

"What do you mean?" I ask, but get no answer and don't press the matter. When we are seated in a banquette at the restaurant, after Quentin has been greeted by a number of his influential advertising friends, along with a few movie stars and sports figures, he gives me the good news.

"You are now a vice president. What do you have to say to that?"

This is a surprise and I'm speechless.

"Say something or he'll take it back," Julie laughs.

Quentin is more like a big brother than a boss. He's done a lot for me and I feel special. Still, I can't help wondering about the guy on the street, Maxwell Baker.

Was Quentin a big brother to him, too?

-48-

After Quentin's approval of the Biggah scripts, the only thing left is for the client to buy the campaign.

At first we're not so sure he will. He complains he's been waiting since June (long before my time) for a TV campaign and here it is months later. He's as loud and threatening as he was after Guy's abysmal efforts.

Julie is again a master at presenting. There's no way of knowing she's battling a life-threatening illness. Healy and Rick and I throw in additional comments as if we're back up singers.

It's apparent that the client is far more interested in the pertinent selling points of the spots than he is in the humor. He emits only the occasional, almost imperceptible snort.

"That's his version of hysterical laughter," Nikki whispers in my ear.

Julie finishes presenting and before the client can comment one way or the other, Bruce, head of TV production, gives the logistical information, talking schedules and budgets. Then there's a short pause for private powwowing on the part of the client and his people, while we on the agency side hold our breaths. Finally, there is the official approval of the campaign.

One thing I have to say about clients is that, aside from their frequent shortcomings, they have to be amongst the bravest people on earth. They can never really know if a campaign will be successful or whether the money they've invested will be wasted. Would I be as trusting if I were a client? So much depends on exactly the right message, public taste and even luck.

With the sale of the campaign secure, we segue into less important issues, such as product identification. Rick holds up the updated package design with "Biggah" in bold type, and the name of the particular item in smaller type.

"I think Biggah should be bigger," someone on the client side says.

"I think Biggah should be smaller," someone else on the client side argues. There's a discussion on this matter going on between the client and his people that takes two full hours. This is forty-five minutes longer than it took for them to buy the campaign. I've been in meetings where one word was discussed for days.

Finally, the boss makes the decision. "The Biggah name will be in red." And that's that.

It takes us about two weeks to complete the pre-prep, most of which is Nikki's responsibility. That means contracting the right director, production company, music people and cast. Securing the studio is one of the thousand other details. When everything is ready, Julie and I are on our way to L.A. to shoot the spots.

At Burbank Airport, I rent a car. We travel the Ventura Freeway, exiting at Laurel Canyon. From there, it's a right turn onto Ventura Boulevard till we come to the Sportsman's Lodge on the right. We take two rooms so as to keep the gossip down, but don't *use* two rooms. Work begins in the morning.

-49-

We're filming on the Paramount Pictures lot, where we may as well be making a full-length, feature film, for all the work that goes into making a 30-second TV commercial. That's because many of the same elements that go into making a full-length feature go into making a 30-second TV spot.

Anyone who thinks that making a movie or a TV commercial is a glamorous undertaking should be present when the sets are being assembled and the lights are being adjusted. These are long, boring periods when we're just sitting around for hours in freezing sound stages. Then, finally, when the director has everything he wants in place, we're ready to shoot, the actors are primed, filming begins, and it can be at ten at night.

Heedless of the budget, a perfectionist director can shoot take after take. Meanwhile, the agency producers, in this case, Nikki and her boss, Bruce, and the production-house producer, can be seen pulling their hair out due to the very costly overtime.

There's often interference from the client. He or she will detect the nit-pickiest thing, something nobody else in a million years would notice, and won't be satisfied until the entire scene is reshot.

In the middle of all this, Nikki and Bruce, who flew out three days early to get things started, are running around doing a dozen other producer jobs.

One of those jobs is to calm rampaging actor/actress egos, especially if the ego belongs to a tempestuous former star. Such is the situation with Vraqqa Bolteck, a one-time, glamorous leading lady from Rumania who made it big in Hollywood, but is now hardly in demand. She's playing the mom in the marriage spot.

"I'm too young to play a mother," she complains.

"Then why did you accept the part?" Nikki asks.

"Money, dahlink, money. I'm getting paid more for doing this stupid commercial than I got for my starring role in "The Lady and the Law-Enforcer.""

Vraqqa wasn't our first choice. Maja, her equally tempestuous twin sister, was offered the script first. Currently starring in a popular TV series, her response to the script was to immediately toss it in the wastepaper basket.

What we didn't know when we hired Vraqqa is that she is a total alcoholic. By eleven in the morning she is looped on her own supply of vodka and is slurring her words. She needs black coffee poured down her throat. If that doesn't help, we will have to let her go and find a replacement. Which is not as easy as it sounds because Miss Bolteck has an ironclad contract.

An embarrassing scene takes place concerning the client's wife, who accompanied her husband to LA. Claiming to know Vraqqa, she goes up to her, extending her hand which Vraqqa simply regards as she would a dead fish.

"I don't know dish woman," Vraqqa announces loudly to the world, humiliating the client's wife and enraging the client.

I'm getting pretty good handling drunks like Vraqqa, so I take it upon myself to walk her around the Paramount lot trying to talk some sense into her about not drinking for the duration of the filming.

"Whosh drinking?"

Three times around the grounds and she's a just a tiny bit more sober. "So you really don't know the client's wife?" I ask.

"Of course I know her. She was my besht friend when we went to finishing shool in Schwizzerland."

"Then why did you say you didn't know her?"

"Becaush, dahlink," Vraqqa says, "Look at her. She looksh

a hundred yearsh old. We're the shame age. If people knew we were in the shame clash at shool, they wouldsh put two and two together and know how old *I* am!"

The next thing that happens is even more bizarre. Maja, furious that Vraqqa has accepted a part that she was originally offered, suddenly wants it back. It's when she arrives on the set unannounced and takes a gun out of her handbag and points it at everyone that things get tense.

"You bitch!" Maja says, now lining up the barrel toward Vraqqa.

"Oh, Maja, jusht go home," Vraqqa says, hardly paying attention to her sister. It's only after the security guards have put their own lives in jeopardy while disarming Maja, and have deposited her into a waiting police ambulance, that the episode is over. Keeping it hush-hush from the tabloids will be another matter.

Despite all the drama, the production of the spot is finally a wrap after two days. Getting the other Biggah commercials made keeps us busy a further three weeks. Then there's the editing in Hollywood.

Julie has to be in Boston for her treatments every Friday. She wants to stay with us in California, but I won't let her do that. "These are my commercials and I'm going to stay here and make sure nobody fucks them up!" Julie fumes.

I'm not surprised at her behavior. Everyone knows her first love in life is the ad game. When I ask her why she loves it so much, she snarls "I just love it, okay? Any further questions?"

She finally agrees to return to Boston, but with proviso number one that she be allowed to return right after her treatment each week and proviso two that I don't sleep with the script girl.

I agree. Julie saved the day with these commercials. She deserves to be treated like the countess that she is.

-50-

The commercials air right away and though it's too early in the proceedings to know how consumers will respond, we feel very good about them.

Everything in the agency is really good, at least for a while. Then Healy throws a wrench in the works. He's had an offer from another agency for more money, so I have to increase his salary in order to keep him. But I want him to earn it. I offer him the job of copy chief and he accepts.

Next problem is the always-joking, good-natured, Rick. When he finds out about Healy's raise and promotion, he's not so good-natured anymore and he's definitely not joking. I have to raise his salary and give him a promotion, too. He becomes the head of the art department.

On the heels of all that, comes Bruce, head of television, who is yelping because we went over the budget to the tune of $52,000 making the Biggah commercials. He's being blamed for it by the Biggah client, who refuses to pay.

Then there's Julie. Even though Allie doesn't want me in her life anymore, I still feel guilty being with another woman, especially one like Julie. My sympathy for her has led to a full-out affair to rival, but hardly surpass, the relationship she has with advertising.

One night, I am awakened by a click, click, click, and when I peer into the darkness of the room, I see Julie, naked and silhouetted against a dimly lit lamp. She tells me to go back to sleep, that she's writing a radio commercial.

Finally, there's Quentin. He's on the phone one morning telling me to pack a bag, that we're going to New Zealand. "It's you and me, kid. I decided to see if I still have what it takes to come up with a fabulous campaign so I did one for Palmer's Paint. Wrote and art- directed it myself, and today I sold it to the head guy."

"Why New Zealand?"

"The scenery. Everywhere you look, you have breathtaking beauty. There are majestic glaciers, tropical beaches, lakes, mountains and waterfalls like you've never seen. This is perfect for a product that creates beauty with a gallon of paint and a paintbrush."

Quentin proceeds to describe the premise of the spots. "These are going to be the first surrealistic TV commercials in history. We've had surrealistic painting, music, even literature, but never surrealistic television commercials. They will be revolutionary."

I don't know if Quentin is trying to convince me, or himself. I let him go on without interruption. Maybe if he talks it out, he'll abandon the idea, which to me, sounds awful.

"Look at what Magritte and Dali and Duchamp accomplished with their paintings. Look at how Freud influenced the field of psychology with his work on dreams, and Man Ray with photography. Dreams are the ultimate surrealistic experience. This is a campaign based on dreams, and aspirations, on wanting to see something appear that no one ever thought possible."

Palmer's Paint is a premium product, considered the best on the market with a price tag to match. At a pre-production meeting in New York, Quentin shows me the scripts he's been working on. I hate them. They are surreal, as he has said, but to me, they're just plain corny, the kind of thing AAB/New York is known for.

"So what do you think, kid?"

"I'm not crazy about them."

"That's okay. You'll change your mind when you see the finished product. We leave a week from tomorrow and you'll be working side by side with me, getting these incredible ideas on film."

When I tell Rick about it and describe what Quentin has in mind, he has a good laugh. "I'm glad it's you and not me that has to work on that stuff."

-51-

I'm beginning to wonder if Quentin can differentiate between good and bad advertising. I mean, can he tell the difference between the kind of work we do in Boston and the stuff that comes out of New York? How come he allows us in Boston to do the kind of work we do? Beats me.

One of his scripts features a young couple getting ready to paint a living room wall in their modest bungalow. They are using Palmer's Magic Matt. The moment their paint brushes touch the wall, they suddenly find themselves atop a glacier (which is why the trip to New Zealand) with the paint brushes still in their hands. The house is no longer modest, but a mansion. They, of course, look surprised out of their minds.

This campaign assumes that the consumer is unfathomably gullible and can be transported to a glacier on the top of the world simply by buying this product. That an ordinary house can be transformed into the Taj Mahal as if by magic.

Hence the theme line Quentin has asked me to write: *Transforms everything it touches.* I've written it and though it's not a bad line, I feel like a tenth-rate hack.

In general, it doesn't make me feel good working on this product. Aside from the lack of believability, I reject it on the grounds that it is inherently dishonest. The truth is, I abhor most of the ads Quentin is known for, even if his theme lines have become part of the American lexicon and have made him famous.

"Put some zip in your sip" for Mackeson's Coffee, and "What's for supper, Ma?" for Larson's Pork and Beans are just two of those theme lines.

I want to tell Quentin that this surrealistic approach is really bad. There was a time when I would have done just that and been fired, but because John has basically given me his friendship and his support, not to mention one last chance to make good, I decide to let it go. We fly to Christchurch on New Zealand's South Island, and the more I am involved the unhappier I get. I keep thinking of the people I worked with at Delehanty, Kurnit and Geller, and the low opinion they would have of me for what I'm doing.

Quentin's energy is boundless. On our first day, he has us up long before dawn. "Okay you guys," he says, banging on our doors at the hotel. "On your feet. We've got work to do."

We quickly assemble, cast and crew, including the director Malcolm Malroon, who specializes in making commercials that look good and say nothing.

In no time at all, we're in vans going way over the speed limit to our first location: Mount Hutt. This is where we will shoot the sun coming up over a specially constructed plinth that sits on the edge of a precipice, spelling out the word Palmer's in big block letters.

Sitting on the plinth is a well-groomed white poodle named Henry. What a white poodle has to do with paint, I do not fucking know, but there has been a white poodle in every print ad and TV spot since the company began.

Henry's frantic female owner makes everyone nervous, including Henry, with her endless, fearful whimpers. When he leaps off the platform into the valley 7,185 feet below, the woman goes completely berserk, her screams echoing in the chilly early morning air.

But the dog hasn't fallen to its death. It is swinging by a leash around its neck and is about to choke to death instead. More screams erupt from the owner. Two or three assistants fish up the almost-hanged dog. It takes Quentin and Malroon a while to placate the hysterical dog owner. They practically have to hold her down so she won't take her dog and leave. Without the dog, there is no shot.

The cameras are soon rolling. It's a race against time, because if the sun rises too high, the shot won't work. Henry's job is to just sit there quietly, an almost impossible task because his owner keeps calling him, telling him that he is a star. There isn't a person present who doesn't want to gag her.

Luckily, we get the shot just before the dog lifts a leg and urinates on the product name.

Meanwhile, I'm put in charge of filming the main visual for a second spot. This one calls for a different location with a door coming out of lake Manipouri, its shiny surface suggesting the deep, thick, luscious, Palmer's Mirror Gloss. If Quentin thinks I'm going to spend the day in a wetsuit in that freezing lake, he is out of his mind.

Quentin tries to talk me back into it, and I tell him I might just be taking the next plane back to Boston if he doesn't let up on the idea of my becoming a frogman. Quentin employs his famous charm act to get me to do what he wants, but I'm adamant I'm not going in that water.

By day five, Malroon won't do what Quentin wants, either. There's a big ultimatum with Malroon telling Quentin to go fuck himself and then quitting the production, leaving Quentin to direct the commercials himself. This is what Quentin has wanted all along, to be in total charge.

He's happily into his element as writer and director. When shown Polaroids of further locations taken by an advanced search party, Quentin orders a small plane to take the two of us all over New Zealand on a "reccy," short for "reconnaissance."

We leave at four each morning, so there's no time for breakfast. By ten minutes past four, I am throwing up in a sick bag. Our flights are like this until it occurs to me to take some bread from dinner the night before and eat it before I get on the plane.

During this time of exploring locations, Quentin and I are like young kids, enjoying the adventure. When we're not traveling by plane, we're driving at 100 miles an hour. In fact, at one point, a New Zealand cop chases us for 160 miles, finally catching up as we get to Aoraki, and issuing a ticket we'll never pay. Nikki and our crew are already at the base camp in a tent waiting for us.

New Zealand's scenery is everything Quentin said it was. Mount Tasman offers all the glacier shots we need. The carpenters are helicoptered up the 11,000 feet to construct a living-room set. Next day, the rest of us are helicoptered up, the agency people, production people, camera crew, and the models acting as the young couple.

The models, not used to waiting around on a high peak in New Zealand, have to remove their parkas for the actual filming, and almost freeze their asses off because they appear in jeans and T-shirts.

This is the first of the disasters. There are many to come, from a batch of flawed film to cameras freezing, to the somewhat less serious case of a driver running over the makeup lady's cosmetic case in the parking lot below.

"You've destroyed my case," the makeup lady screams. "Everything is ruined."

"Oh sure," the driver says. "All dem powder puffs."

After this spot is finally filmed, Nikki and I make sure the young couple, suffering from hypothermia, is safely transported to a hospital in Christchurch (something Quentin doesn't seem at all concerned about), and we move on to the last location. This is at the astonishingly beautiful Milford Sound, and then finally, we are done. All the spots are in the can, and we depart for the United States.

When we get to Hollywood for editing, I see the footage is just as I thought it would be: Incredibly gorgeous with all that majestic New Zealand scenery, but lacking believability. The spots are the exact opposite of what good advertising is all about.

-52-

Back in Boston, I fall into a deep depression. After years of getting canned because I wouldn't work on blatantly dishonest projects, I've wound up doing just that.

Not that I came up with those scripts, but I did write the tagline. And in LA, I tightened up the copy as Quentin requested.

Now, I just want to hole up, see no one. Not even Julie-- especially not Julie. Then the phone rings. "You're back and you didn't tell me?

When Julie cools down, she offers to drive out to Brookline Village and spend the night with me. I tell her I'm too tired from the trip. So she makes a big fuss about never sleeping at my house. I had told her, several times in fact, that I prefer not to make love in Allie's and my bed. I feel bad enough for having done so with her before.

"So the bed your wife slept in is now a sacred shrine?" she complains.

No one else ever sees this side of Julie, the dark side. In the office, she's always bright and apparently happy, always wearing a mantle of courage about her. She continues to have everyone's sympathy, although mine is wearing thin.

I wish I could leave town again, even if it means attending one of those blasted focus groups. Having to listen to farmers in the Midwest and housewives in Phoenix giving their opinions, as if they were experts in advertising, is a form of slow torture. They've probably never been asked an opinion in their lives. Now, six dollars and all the peanuts they can eat, they're encouraged to talk on and on about what they like and what they don't like about a certain product.

Unfortunately, the more inane their statements, the more influential they are in dictating the direction an agency will take in creating campaigns. This isn't supposed to happen, but is exactly what *does* happen.

The Creative Revolution, mainly initiated by Doyle, Dane Bernbach, with the brilliant Alka Seltzer and Volkswagen ads, relied on the instincts of the writers and art directors who created them. Focus groups represent a threat to this phenomenon.

Account executives, traditionally viewed as glorified errand boys, are always on the lookout for ways to wrest power from creative people, and research seems to be their main weapon. "To hell with trusting the natural instincts of a copywriter or art direction," they say. "This is the age of research!"

No matter how copywriters and art directors in agencies across America fight this, there's a general feeling of defeat even before war with the account execs is declared.

-53-

Carl Mayler has a request. His wife, he says, hates being separated from him. "She looks so sad when I go to work in the morning. And it's not like she can hang out with friends, because she doesn't have any in Boston—so she's lonely and unhappy. So look, would it be all right if she came to work with me every day? She wouldn't bother anyone. She would just sit quietly in a corner and read a book or something. You wouldn't even know she was there."

"You're kidding, right?" I ask.

"Honestly, Bob, this won't be forever. Just till she gets used to living here."

This is totally nuts, completely out of the question, but I have an idea. "I hear there's an opening for a clerk in the mailroom."

It isn't long before Sheila is hired as the new mailroom girl. She takes her job seriously, saying ours will be the best mailroom in Boston. She makes it her business to know everyone in every department, as well as every event on the agency calendar, including every important meeting.

It's during one of the important meetings for Gunderschlaken Sparkling Wine when a very strange thing happens. We're settled in the conference room and the creative team, Carl and Healy, are just about to present when the door opens and we all turn around.

"Hi everyone," Sheila says brightly while pushing her cart. "Don't let me bother you. I'm taking a break from the back-breaking job of delivering mail and I thought I would join you."

I watch in amazement as Sheila approaches us at the conference room table and takes a seat.

"Carry on," Sheila says, "don't let me interrupt you. I'm just resting the old tootsies."

This is beyond belief. I say nothing and do nothing, knowing it will only make matters worse if I chase Sheila out of the room. But I am going to have it out with Carl right after the meeting, that's for sure.

Carl looks like he's about to have a heart attack. "Shall we begin?" he says with a shaky voice and sickly smile.

"In this commercial," he starts, pointing to the first frame of a storyboard, "we're at a dinner party, and after a toast, the attendees are raising their glasses of Gunderschlaken sparkling wine to their lips. You can hear the bubbles. They're very loud, drowning out all conversation. That's the whole funny concept for these spots, the loud bubbles."

"Very interesting," Sheila interrupts, "but may I make a suggestion?" She doesn't wait for anyone to grant her permission, but jumps right in. "Instead of these people bringing the glasses to their lips, they should bring them to their ears."

Healy, Carl, and I just stare at Sheila. I can't believe she has dared to open her mouth in this presentation, especially by saying something so incredibly off the wall. Bringing the glasses to their ears? But the more I think about it, that's not so off the wall. In fact, it's a great idea. The client, at this point, has shifted his entire attention to Sheila.

Carl jumps up and speaks before Sheila can say anything else. "This works perfectly with all the noise the bubbles are making and the theme line: *Enjoy a glass of Gunderschlaken tonight.*"

"No, no, no," Sheila says, "that line stinks. It should be: *Listen to a glass of Gunderschlacken tonight*. Makes more sense. Right? Then the voiceover can talk about how our grapes are better than that ritzy French crap."

"It's a theme line that will lend itself to print ads, TV spots. Billboards, and radio spots," Healy interjects, trying to keep up with Sheila.

We're all waiting for the client to react negatively to the idea, but he says the concept is a departure from the old and certainly is different.

"It's an ear-opener," he says and then falls into gales of laughter at his own pun. And then he looks directly at Sheila and in a serious tone, asks her what she would suggest to get the product better known.

"Let's face it," Sheila begins, "you're looking to boost sales for a brand lost in a category rife with exclusive and super-premium sparkling wines. You need to give purpose and meaning to a new audience in the U.S. and the rest of the world. I would suggest you put all your advertising dollars into more broadcasting time and less into trade press space."

Sheila sounds, much to the amazement of Carl, Healy, and myself, like an experienced product-analyst. "Take my word for it, a smart move like that will get you a higher percentage of market share."

This is Sheila? First she takes over the meeting as a creative force, and now she's giving the client marketing advice? I look over at the client who is concentrating intently on every word Sheila is saying. And everything Sheila says is astounding.

"And since this is an alcoholic beverage," she continues, "it would be revolutionary to add a 'If you drink, don't drive' line at the end of each spot."

Where did Sheila get that idea? It's totally original. Did it come out of her head just now? It's brilliant.

"Young lady," the client addresses Sheila, "you've come up with a number of fresh ideas. Not just in the execution of the campaign, but in the selling of the brand. All together, it's sure to get a lot of people talking. Imagine that, listening to a glass of Gunderschlaken!" And with that he falls into gales of laughter again.

"Glad you like it," Sheila says, "and by the way, folks, that name, Gunderschlaken? It has to go. Have you ever thought of calling it something people can pronounce?"

-54-

Later, everyone, especially Carl, wants to know where Sheila got her creative and marketing expertise.

"What do you think I've been doing, just sitting in the mail room sorting out the mail? I've been reading *Advertising Age* like a maniac. And maybe you haven't noticed, but I'm not reading all that romance junk like I usually do, but have got a whole lot of books out of the library on effective advertising. I'm getting quite an education."

Based on her performance with the Gunderschlaken client, and the fact that the client has upped the frequency of the TV campaign dollars from twice a night to four times, I take her out of the mailroom and make her a cub writer in the creative department. And the first art director she gets to work with is her own husband, Carl.

Everything goes well with them for a couple of days until Carl comes to see me. "I can't work with her. She's driving me nuts. She hates my layouts, she hates my choice of typefaces, she hates my suggestions. She's like Hitler!"

She may be driving Carl nuts, but her ideas are extraordinary, some of the best in the agency. To increase subscription sales for the Boston Light Opera, she has written the line: "Reserve the Edge of Your Seats." And for a local politician campaigning against an allegedly-corrupt opponent: "Don't believe every *true* story you hear."

All this has made Sheila more of a prima donna than she was before. Not only with Carl, but everyone else in the agency, demanding—and getting—her way in almost everything, from what accounts she will work on and won't, to challenging clients to give in to her innovative ideas or find somebody else to work on their accounts.

As successful as Sheila may be, there's a lot of controversy over the ads Abraham Washington, still a cub writer, has been turning out. The account people just don't like them. This is a case of thinly-veiled resentment toward Abraham due to his color.

The only beef I have has to do with him never getting to work on time. I remember the scene at the elevator banks when Ridgeley tore into him for being late in picking him up. All my efforts to get him in the office by nine in the morning have failed, but he more than makes up for it by working late into the night, so I let it pass.

After he has been trained on lesser important work—brochures and trade ads—I try him on our Iceland Travel account. With Nelson as his mentor, guide and art director, he has come up with "See Iceland before it Melts," an ad that makes all of us laugh. All of us, that is, with the exception of Tod Lawson, who comes unannounced to my office, trailed by Lorne Chambers, who obsequiously agrees with everything Tod thinks, says and does.

"I've been against that truly ridiculous *See Iceland before it Melts* ad from the start," Tod says. "We all know Iceland could never melt, that it will stay frozen for another hundred billion years".

"And we don't like the honeymoon ad," Lorne reminds his boss, eliciting from me the strong desire to kick his ass down the hall.

He's referring to a double-page spread for newly married couples considering Iceland as a honeymoon destination, also authored by Abraham: *We give Honeymooners a lot More to Explore than Just Each Other.*

I address Tod, ignoring Lorne: "What don't you like about it?"

"It's obscene," he says.

"Well, what do you think honeymooners do on their honeymoons, read books?" I reply.

Another of Abraham's headlines, *All the Benefits of Upcountry Living and none of the Manure* is for a housing development in the middle of cattle-raising country about forty miles southeast of Dallas. Tod is even more vociferous over this headline than *See Iceland before it Melts* and *We give honeymooners a Lot More to Explore than Just Each Other.*

"I simply will not allow the word 'manure' to be used in any of my ads," he explodes.

"Fine," I say, "we'll just replace it with the word 'shit.' "

The "manure" ad is instantly loved by the client, but Abraham has not been invited to any of the client presentations.

And then, when I officially make Abraham a full copywriter--his tenure as a cub writer being only slightly longer than Sheila's—I get a blast of bigotry from Tod.

Tod raises hell when he gets the memo about Abraham's promotion. He demands to know what I'm planning to do when it's time to present work to the clients.

"Well, if you want to know, Tod, I'm planning for him to be included in all client meetings and not only that, he will personally introduce his work to the clients."

"And you really, really think you can get away with insulting our clients by having a *negro* in the very same room with them? Well *I'm* the acting managing director and as such, I am issuing a direct order that you either hide this person where no one will see him, or get rid of him!"

"I have a better idea," I say. "Let's march him out to Copley Square and lynch him."

Though it has never been articulated to my face, I know that Tod would have me hanging from the gallows next to Abraham's, being that I am a Jew.

As soon as Tod leaves my office, I assign Abraham to three of his accounts.

-55-

Just because pilgrims landed on these shores nearly 350 years ago, and supposedly had that huge feast with the natives, we have to go through the tiresome, yearly ritual known as Thanksgiving, ranking only second to the insanity of Christmas.

Any holiday right now is hard to take, especially with my family breakup. The prospect of seeing Allie, however, if just for a brief moment when I pick up the kids, is making me light-headed with joy.

There's one problem: Julie. I never thought to tell her what I'll be doing on Thanksgiving, but when I casually mention I'm spending the day with my kids, she immediately brightens.

"Great," she says, "I can't wait to meet them. I love kids."

Julie has misunderstood me and thinks she is included in my Thanksgiving plans. This is taking an awkward turn.

"Julie, my kids are still reacting to the separation. To bring a friend up with me would only confuse them."

"So what you're saying is that you don't want me to meet your kids? Is that it?"

I say nothing. There's nothing to say.

"And what about your wife?" she asks.

"My wife?"

"Yeah, your W.I.F.E. Maybe you don't want her to know about me. Maybe it's not just the kids."

What Julie says is absolutely true. I *don't* want Allie to know about her. I don't want her to *even suspect* that there might be someone else.

"Are you going to deny it?" Julie asks.

"Look, Julie, calm down," I say. "I'm sorry it won't work out for you to be with us on Thanksgiving. But we can have the day after."

"The hell the day after!" Julie says. I'm not all that surprised at her outburst. She's been "acting out" a lot recently. *The poor kid*, I think. She has a terrible disease and might die. I feel like a bastard.

I'm on the verge of giving in to her about joining the kids and me, bizarre as that would be, but I can't get the words out. I envision what Allie would think, not to mention my kids. I can see them looking up and asking: "Who is this woman with the big red lips? Why aren't you with Mommy?" I can't do that to them.

-56-

Arrangements have been finalized. I'm to arrive around noon, pick up the kids and take them out for lunch.

Much as I think of Thanksgiving as morbid, it is still family time, and when I think about my family, I automatically include Allie. We may never again live as man and wife, but she is my family, and always will be.

I haven't seen her or the kids for weeks, and when I get to the house, I fully expect Beryl to bar me from entering, but it's Allie who comes to the door. Beryl, she says, has the kids out for a walk to the harbor.

She looks serene. Her eyes are clear and her voice isn't shaky. I realize she doesn't know anything about the success I'm having as creative director of AAB/Boston. When I tell her, she kisses me quickly on the cheek. This is a totally unexpected gift that almost makes me high.

"I'm glad you've come. You've promised a few times, and then never came." There's no hint of an accusation in Allie's tone. But I can tell that I disappointed the kids, and maybe her.

"It was work and deadlines. Couldn't be helped. I should have phoned."

"Hey," Allie says, brightly, "you can't be married to an advertising man for as long as I was and not grow accustomed to being stood up." She tries to laugh but doesn't succeed. She spent too many years with a bottle instead of a husband. Already some of her brightness is starting to fade.

We sit there with a lot of silence between statements, both

aware of how dampened our spirits have suddenly become. When Beryl returns with the kids, her sarcasm doesn't help matters.

"So it's the devoted father," she says sourly. Angela and Stephen come rushing over to me and I cling to then for a very long time. Picking up little Charlie, I bounce him on my knee. He probably doesn't even remember me.

"Are you taking us home, Daddy?" Angela asks. "Not this time, Honey," I say, handing her the doll I brought, and giving Stephen toy soldiers I know he'll like. Angela helps him get them out of the box.

"Six German soldiers, one bleeding," Angela says, taking in-ventory. "One U-Boat captain."

"They're growing up fast," I say to Allie.

"In a couple of weeks, Charlie starts to shave," Beryl says, standing there with one hand on her hip.

"I don't get you, Beryl," I say. "First you make cracks when I come to see my kids, and now you complain I don't come enough."

"Who's complaining? You aren't worth a complaint."

"Please, you two," Allie says. "Don't speak—just leave each other alone." The old tension is back in the room, thanks to Beryl.

"I'll take the kids out for a bit," I say.

"They've just been out for a bit," Beryl says. "They don't need pneumonia."

"Would it be all right with you if I took them for a ride in the car then?" I ask Beryl with equal sarcasm.

"Should I put their coats on again?" Allie asks, looking from Beryl to me, the old haunted look on her face.

"Please," I say.

"Is it okay if I go with you?" Again, a feeling of elation washes over me. In few minutes, Allie, the kids and I are heading up to Maine. In Kittery Point we stop at a restaurant for Thanksgiving lunch. It occurs to me that we look like your average family, but we're only masquerading as one. Then we drive to a long stretch of beach and get out of the car. Angela takes baby Charlie in her very capable, seven-year old hands and they go off a short way to play in the sand, Stephen following. That leaves Allie and me alone for a few minutes.

"What's going to happen?" Allie asks.

"What do you want to happen?" I reply.

"I don't know," Allie says. "I just don't know. Beryl is so uptight when you visit, and the kids need to see you. I just don't know."

"What if I asked you to move back with me?" In the back of my mind I have an image of Julie, and a vast sea of confusion swamps me. I look at Allie who, like me, is torn.

"I can't," Allie finally says. "Maybe someday, but not now. Ever since we got married, everything revolved around you and your jobs. It was like I didn't matter. Now I do matter, to me, anyway. I've got to identify this person I am—learn to live with her. I think what I'm trying to say is that this is my problem, not yours, Bob. I need time."

At this moment, I know Allie is right because what she says is true, that everything revolved around me and she was always walking on eggshells because I might lose a job, which I did regularly. It had to be nerve-wracking for her. I'm so sorry. I take her in my arms and kiss her.

Nearby, the kids are building castles in the sand, and I'm thinking of castles in the sky.

-57-

Castles in the sky, as far as my dreams for being reunited with my family go, are just that. This is the time we should be together, when I'm having some real success for a change with this excellent job, supportive boss, and a creative crew I can depend on. Most importantly, when I'm not trying to destroy everything that's good in my life as I usually do.

Maybe it's because I can get most of our work through without it being screwed up by some asinine account exec or moronic client, that I don't feel the need to challenge anyone. If anything, I feel in control of things and more mature, not given to making ultimatums.

But one thing has to change. I have to end it with Julie because I can never care about her the way she wants me to or the way I care about Allie. I plan to tell her at the earliest opportunity. That never happens. I look at her and just can't do it. It's bad enough she's ill. Adding to that would be an act of incredible cruelty.

Maybe she's reading my mind because one day, apropos of nothing, she suddenly says: "I hope you know that you mean the world to me, and I wouldn't like it if you wanted to break up." From the expression on her face, I feel trapped. I decide to let it ride for now and hope she'll get sick of me.

It's so busy in the agency I don't have time to think about Julie, but when I do, the trapped feeling returns. I concentrate on other things, such as figuring a way to hire more writers and art directors. It's the usual fight to get the money from New York.

Management there is reluctant to release funds for more employees.

I'm lucky in having added Abraham and Sheila to the creative team and having been able to give Rick and Healy raises so they would stay with us. Even with two extra, we're all extremely overloaded, working ungodly hours and rarely taking a lunch break. We're here most nights till after eleven and on weekends. Enormous creative energy goes into our endeavors. The place is like a dream factory as we turn out one sensational ad or commercial after another. No one complains—we're having too much fun.

Fun or not, we're starting to show signs of fatigue. Finally, I get a budget to hire some more people. I decide to sidestep Bunny Berger and do what most creative directors do to get people. Steal them. From a somewhat creative boutique agency in Boston, I steal copywriter Rob Hewitt and art director Paul Wolfman.

They're not the most talented people in the world, but probably the best Boston has to offer, which isn't saying much. My hope is that they will grow into their jobs and become sensational. They accept immediately.

AAB/Boston has become *the* place to work, who wouldn't accept? Writer Amy Marshfield, to name one. She's a heavyweight I would like to have, someone I already know from my last agency, the only person who didn't condemn me for destroying the client's portrait.

"Hell," she had said at the time, "I would have done the same thing if he had walked all over my ads, and I would have given him a bonus kick in the you-know-what."

I like that about Amy: She has your back. A tall and striking-looking twenty-six year-old blonde, she's also a health nut who's into something called "New Age." She chants and meditates each day, stuff most people have never heard of.

It's apparent that she's part of a movement the media has labeled Women's Lib and you don't want to get her started on that subject. In terms of her skills as a copywriter, she is one of the best. Clients don't usually care who creates their ads—many of us are just forgettable faces, but Amy's clients adore her.

A few days after the Thanksgiving break, I ask her to stop up at my office so I can talk to her about coming to the agency. She keeps the appointment, but it doesn't look like she'll switch agencies. "I couldn't leave my clients in the lurch. They depend on me. We're like family."

"Bring them with you," I suggest.

"You're kidding, right?" Amy asks.

"No, I'm not. They'd probably follow you wherever you go. You could come to AAB/Boston and practically have your own agency within an agency, without all the overheads." Although I don't say it to Amy, the agency would undoubtedly benefit from the extra revenue.

"Sounds interesting, but I wouldn't even consider coming if I wasn't getting the same money as the guys. I don't believe that a woman should get a penny less than a man. Women have been buying that bullshit for far too long."

"I wouldn't be able to give you the same," I say.

"Well, in that case, see you around."

"I'd have to give you more. You're worth it."

When she laughs out loud, I know we have a deal. We discuss terms, and the starting date and other particulars. Getting up to leave, she walks around the desk to give me one of her big bear-hugs. It's a totally platonic thing. There are some women who, no matter how sexy or beautiful, are like sisters.

It doesn't look much like brother and sister to Julie, who unexpectedly walks in, and out, slamming the door behind her.

-58-

That slammed door means a fight coming up. They're getting more and more frequent. As always, I've been attributing her flaring temper to her disease, but there's obviously more to it. If it wasn't for her being ill and all, I would sever the tie, but I'm starting to feel like I don't give a damn if she walks out. In fact, I think I would welcome it.

To get on with my job as creative director, I have to sidestep personal problems. I wish I could also sidestep some of our clients. They get pretty nasty when it involves dwindling profits or less than effective advertising. And it doesn't help when the client just so happens to be a major prick like the managing director of MassAssurance Investments, Arnold Schwirp. He doesn't look happy when we meet today to discuss the strategy for his new campaign. In the same way Biggah had been discontent with the advertising done by Ridgeley and his crew, the same is true of Schwirp.

More than that, Schwirp has notified us by letter that he's invited other agencies to pitch the business, but as a courtesy, is allowing us the chance, slim though it is, to try and keep the account. This is such an important account for AAB that the New York office has sent its ultimate salesman, John Quentin, to deal with it. He's incredible to watch in action.

Considering he only had several days notice, I don't know how he found time to prepare for the pitch. He's done it with the help of the head office account and research departments that have put together a formidable presentation. Using charts and graphs on a screen, Quentin discusses the target market demographics, market trends and growth statistics over the past two years.

His approach is one of honesty. He admits that past campaigns, though successful, haven't really connected with the consumer in the dynamic way they were intended. He touches on eight years of work, showing the positives as best as possible. Additionally, he compares the campaigns of various competitors, a critique that's not exactly complimentary to those companies, but instructive in terms of what we are doing right and wrong. Finally, he gives a detailed overview of what AAB/ Boston can do for them.

As the highly-informed and persuasive presenter he is known to be, Quentin delves deep into MassAssurance so thoroughly as to impress everyone in the room. Everyone, that is, except Arnold Schwirp.

"Hell," Schwirp says, cutting Quentin off, "you haven't told me one thing I don't already know. *I am the managing director of MassAssurance Investments, you know.*" He then goes on at length, telling us how he makes it his business to be extremely astute in terms of knowing everything about his company and the market.

"As I told you before, I'm allowing you to re-pitch the business," he says, "but I don't want to sit here and hear all the same old claptrap. I want to hear solutions that will increase our slice of the investment business, and so far I haven't heard a damn thing that's new, fresh or different!"

It makes me uncomfortable that John is being chastised by this razor-tongued creep. Quentin doesn't look ruffled, however. He's used to nasty clients.

"Well, Arnold, I think we can accommodate you. You are discontented because of work done under our former creative director. We have remedied that situation by bringing in a new creative director whose work is fresh and innovative. The New York office is confident this move will guarantee our clients the most effective campaigns we've ever executed."

Schwirp looks even more irritated by this statement. "I can assure you, that the reason I am giving AAB/Boston a second chance has absolutely nothing whatsoever to do with your New York office, or for that matter, you. It has to do with what I'm hearing about the new creative people here, such as Mr. Bronson."

What's happening is not my fault, but I feel like it is. It's very awkward. Please, I pray, don't let this jerk say anything that's complimentary about AAB/Boston's creative department or me. But the guy just won't shut up.

"If Mr. Bronson here can do for me what he's done for some of his other clients, I might be willing to extend our contract."

As usual, I find myself unable to keep quiet. "Mr. Schwirp," I say, "I appreciate your faith in my abilities, but it's Mr. Quentin's remarkable vision that allows for the kind of creativity that has impressed you." I don't know about my usage of the word 'vision,' but it is definitely true that John lets us do great work.

When the meeting is finally over, Schwirp announces he'll inform us in due course whether he will keep us on. My feeling is he will keep us, but it's obvious that it's not because of John, who continues his pleasant demeanor until Schwirp and his people are gone.

Then he turns to look at me with annoyance written all over his face. I had expected him to say something to the effect that it was a lousy meeting and maybe something negative about Schwirp, but that's not the case. His annoyance is directed to me.

"Don't," he says, "you ever, ever, do that again."

Aside from being taken aback by this, I have no idea what he's talking about.

"Do what?" I ask.

"Defend me in public."

-59-

When the telephone rings at two in the morning, all I can think is that there's an emergency in Portsmouth. Maybe one of the kids is ill. But it's nothing like that, thank God.

Instead it's the extremely slurred voice of John Quentin. After his pissed-off mood of yesterday, I'm surprised he's on the phone now. My first thought is that he's going to fire me.

"Hey, old buddy, John Quentin says, now back to being my pal, "I want to apologizsh. I had no right talking to you that way yeshterday. You were being very shuppotive and that's how I repaid you, by giving yoush a hard time."

This guy is always apologizing. He's one of the most apologetic people I've ever known. But it's one of the most likeable things about him. In this business of massive egos, most people in his position wouldn't apologize if it killed them.

However, in the weeks to come, I will look back on that moment in the boardroom, when he showed such annoyance toward me, as the beginning of the end of our relationship. But right now, I'm more understanding. I can see how a mere regional creative director praising someone so much higher on the corporate ladder can be perceived as a form of serious insubordination.

For him to praise me would be perfectly all right, but not the other way around.

"Forget it, John," I tell him "That Schwirp character was completely out of line."

"No he washn't," John says, sounding even drunker than before. "Schwirpsh is a good man. And you're a good man. A very good man. The besht."

"Thanks, John, maybe we can talk about this later on this morning."

John talks on as if he hasn't heard me. "I washn't prepared," he says. "Schwirpsh was right. I wash giving him the shame old crock of shit and he shaw I wash doing that, giving him the shame old crock of shit. He was protecting his compa-n-y while I was letting oursh down."

"Hey, John," I say, "isn't that a bit harsh? Your presentation was great." Soon as I say this, I think *uh oh, I'm doing it again. I'm praising him again.*

Again, it doesn't seem like John has heard me. Talking to a drunk is usually one-sided.

"Let me make it up to you old buddy," Quentin says. "Let me give you a big raizsh. How would you like a big raizsh?"

"John, you don't have to do that. I haven't even been with the agency six months."

"Yesh, but look what you've done in those shix monthsh. Think what you'll do in shix more monthsh. You turned the placsh around. Around. Comp-l-e-t-e-l-y around. You're one of the besht men I know. A geniush. You desherve a raizsh. I'm giving you a raizsh. Ten thousand dollarsh. There, that's shet-tled."

And then there's silence. I'm not sure what's happened to our line. I think John may have passed out. I wait on the line for him to come back, but he doesn't.

I figure he probably won't remember this conversation in the morning. Drunks rarely remember anything they've done the night before.

-60-

Next time I talk to Quentin, which is six hours later, he makes no mention of his middle-of-the-night call. Or the $10,000 'raizsh.'

If anything, he sounds pissed off again. I've given his tendency to sound pissed off a name: A urinary inflection. He wants to know the progress on several campaigns we're working on. He says he expects "a complete report by the end of the week."

To make up for this unpleasantness, I get a call from Amy Marshfield saying she has had talks with her beloved clients, including her biggest, Darlene Snooze & Soothe Overnight Skin Rejuvenation Products, and they told her they're prepared to move with her to AAB/Boston.

These clients are like little baby chicks trailing after their mama. They would probably follow her to the ends of the earth, or so it seems.

Amy could start her own agency with these accounts, and I tell her so. She says she might do that one day, but coming to AAB/Boston will allow her time to pursue her real interests, which happen to be the furthest possible thing from the crazy world of advertising: Personal growth and spiritual enfoldment.

"I believe we come back into each lifetime for a purpose," she tells me. "My purpose this time is to help people grow and be the best they can be." To that end she has, within days of arriving, started her ministry within the creative department as well as with the bullpen staff of typesetters and layout artists.

Whether they like it or not, she has spoken with each of

them about such things as developing self-esteem, remedying sexual dysfunction, the joy of yoga, and benefits of meditation.

She's also on everyone's case about their eating habits, especially those people who are overweight. "I like my food, so leave me alone, willya?" our extremely chubby chief layout artist says.

"And do you like the idea of having a heart attack at the age of thirty?" Amy replies. "Or how about a stroke? You know, one of those strokes where you become a drooling vegetable?"

Amy is a walking advertisement for healthful living. Soon she has people asking her advice on everything from the benefits of fiber in the diet to cures for premature ejaculation. For all her efforts, however, there's one person she can't win over no matter how much she tries. And that's Julie.

"Get thee to a loony bin," Julie says when Amy suggests she start a course of colonics to cure her leukemia. "Why don't you work on curing your need to force unwanted advice on others?" Julie has asked her.

Another irritant for Julie is that, aside from Amy's health preaching, her writing skills and her concepts, headlines and body copy are brilliant. Within a month, Amy is propelled into the same arena as Julie who, up until now, couldn't be toppled from her position as best copywriter of AAB/Boston.

Then Rick comes to see me about her. "We're all walking on eggshells," he says. "I almost got my head handed to me the other day when I just happened to mention that Amy did a very good job on an ad."

The real threat to Julie, as it turns out, isn't Amy, but of all people, short, dumpy Sheila, who has taken the agency by storm, producing one extraordinary ad after another, each with an iron rationale that puts her in a category all her own. No one else, absolutely no one else, even comes close to her.

-61-

As Sheila's importance to the agency grows, so does her list of demands: A window office, furnishings of her choice (which means a shopping tour on Newberry Street) and a hefty raise. She gets all three.

That's not all. She won't work with certain people. This includes her husband whom she regards as a talentless twit--and has said so. I can't help wondering how long it will take for some other agency to come along and offer her twice or three times her salary.

For that matter, I wonder how long we'll have Abraham. The war in Vietnam has flung its tentacles out like grappling hooks, dragging young men to the slaughter. The specter of Abraham being called up is scary, but not half as scary as his attitude.

"If they call me, I'll go. It's my duty to serve my country," Abraham says.

"You wouldn't be serving your country," our anti-Vietnam crusader, Nelson, corrects him. "You'd be serving a bunch of old men in Washington who think nothing of sending young guys off to fight and die."

"Still and all," Abraham insists, "My dad was a Tuskegee Airman during the war. He fought the Nazis with courage and never for a minute thought of running away from his responsibilities. He would never understand if I didn't do the same thing as him. I could never look him in the eye again if I ran. He would say that our country is at war and that it's my duty as an American to serve."

"An African-American," Nelson says, interrupting Abraham. "African-Americans are a minority in this country, but a majority when it comes to the fatalities in Vietnam. In other words, more blacks as a group are being killed than whites."

It doesn't look like facts and figures or anything Nelson says can sway Abraham away from this deadly choice.

"When I get my orders, I will serve," he says, "and I will serve proudly to the victorious end."

Nelson says no more, nor do I.

-62-

The war is the most discussed issue of the day, but it isn't the only battle on our minds. There's one much closer to home, and that's the growing AAB/Boston battle, with the creative people and me on one side, and the accounts department on the other, and the inescapable fact that Lorne is getting more and more powerful each day.

Apparently, he has bagged a large account--Bounty Beer— reinforcing him as the current darling of headquarters in New York. Never before has he been so appreciated by an advertising agency. Everyone has his day; this is Lorne's.

All I know is that I'd like to bash him in the teeth for causing three times the disharmony and difficulty as Powell. Problems erupt in the creative department when both Rick and Healy threaten to quit if Lorne doesn't get off their backs.

"The guy's in my office every two minutes looking over my shoulder, telling me how to do my job," Rick says.

"And now," Healy says, "the creep wants us to do a pro-police ad for the *Times-Informer* supporting police efforts to keep the peace. Can you imagine that?"

Considering the police actions taking place these days, no, I cannot imagine that. I'm against the ad and resolved to do nothing to get such an outrageous and dishonest piece done. A couple of days pass and I've forgotten about it, but Lorne hasn't. He's in my office, rapping on my desk.

"I need that ad," he says sharply. "And I need it pronto."

"Tough shit," is my reply.

"Are you going to take care of this or not?"

"Absolutely not."

"Okay," Lorne says, backing off, "if you're not going to do the ad, I'll do it myself. I'm an excellent copywriter as you know." Another of Lorne's delusions.

Next day he's is back in my office interrupting a planning meeting I'm having with a strangely subdued Nelson, and a still-seething Rick and Healy.

"Thought you might want to see the brilliant ad I wrote for the *Times-Informer.*"

"Wrong," I reply.

"The headline is *What You Should Know About Your Police Department* and the copy talks about how the police are preserving the peace."

"You've gotta be joking," Rick says.

"I'm not joking and you're going to do the layout for me," Lorne says.

"It'll be a cold day in hell before I'll touch it," Rick says, "and you won't find anyone else around here willing to work on it, either."

"The paper is your account, Rick," Lorne says. "You are required to lay out the ads."

"Not this one. I'll quit first."

Realizing he'll never get anywhere with Rick, Lorne relents. "I can always hire a freelancer," he says.

As it turns out, the police ad isn't the only reason Lorne is in my office. He wants to bitch about something else. "I don't like the campaign you guys came up with for the Boston National bank," he says, "and my clients won't like it either. I demand that you kill that idea and come up with something new for me to present next Tuesday."

"That will never happen," I say.

"Oh, I think it will, my friend, and if it isn't me who persuades you, I can assure you it will be someone in New York who will."

"Well, I tell you what, Lorne, we're not going to start all over again. This is the campaign we're presenting, like it or not."

The assignment is to advertise the bank's various benefits. The only drawback is that the bank doesn't have various benefits. It doesn't even have one appreciable benefit. It doesn't do anything extra for a customer beyond what other banks do, and in most cases, it does much less. And its interest rates are higher.

This is where the legendary advertising man, Rosser Reeves, comes to mind. His dictum is to find a product's unique selling point, no matter how insignificant, and to use that as the focus of the ad. This is a rule I make sure is observed in all the work we do. I hate not giving the consumer a reason to buy a product.

We've recently had to do this with a line of Maxwell's Men's Shirts that were so ordinary that the art director and copywriter sat around for days trying to come up with a headline and visual. They finally did come up with something.

All the ad showed were a bunch of covered buttons and the headline: *These are Maxwell's covered buttons. They come with a matching shirt.*

In the same way that we found a solution for Maxwell's making covered buttons seem special, we found a solution for Boston National that says everything and nothing at the same time.

One headline reads: *If we had your money, we'd let us manage it.* Another says: *We help your money make more money.*

This is a good way to make the bank seem like it has an edge, even if it has none. And that being the case, I ask Lorne why he feels we should drop it.

"I don't like it," Lorne says. "It doesn't say anything."

If I was annoyed just talking to Lorne before this, I'm now getting ready to throw him out of my office. "You're the account exec on this account and you haven't given us any selling points to work with, so we've had to invent something, and you now have the nerve to criticize us?"

"Yeah, well," Lorne says, not replying to that charge, "I don't like what you've 'invented,' and I know my friends at the bank won't, either."

"If you want us to change it, you and your 'friends' at the

bank need to provide us with something concrete to go on. We have to give consumers a reason to bank there, and that's what we've done."

"What about talking about free checking? And late nights on Friday, and friendly service?" Lorne asks. "I've given you a ton of information."

"All banks do that," Nelson says, speaking up for the first time. "So you haven't given us shit."

"Listen, you drug addict," Lorne says, "maybe if you weren't high on cocaine and LSD all the time, maybe you'd come up with a decent campaign for the bank."

"And if you weren't such a dumb, useless prick, maybe you would do your job which is to at least pretend to being an account man," Nelson replies. "So why don't you go fuck yourself."

"Hey," Lorne says, turning to me, "he just told me to go fuck myself! I'm a respected account manager and I've just been told by this sleazy druggie to go fuck myself. You are the creative director, so I want an answer from you. What do you have to say about this?"

"I guess there's only thing I can say, which is that Nelson is worth a dozen of you to this agency, and because you are one of the most obnoxious, stupid and despicable people I have ever known, you can go fuck yourself."

"This is war, Lorne says."

"No, buddy, *this* is war," Nelson says, standing up and displaying a fist the size of a grapefruit. "You mouth off one more time and you're going to find your teeth have moved to another continent."

"Are you threatening me?" Lorne asks.

"You bet your ass, I am," Nelson replies. He's been very cool up until now, very controlled, but I can sense he could lose it if pushed any further. "And if you don't go out and sell our bank campaign, you'll find yourself eating gravel." With that, he shoves Lorne so hard, he's sent flying across the room into the wall.

"I'll get you for this," Lorne says. "If it's the last thing I do,

I'll get you. You're going to be very, very sorry. Just you wait." It sounds so ridiculous, like something a child would say. Well, Lorne *is* a child.

"I'm waiting, you little turd," Nelson says.

I applaud Nelson for saying to Lorne what I have wanted to say for so many years. I'm taking him and Rick and Derek to lunch and when we get down to the ground floor after so much discord with Lorne, we're told by the security guard that there's been discord on the street as well--another violent clash between the war protestors and the cops.

Apparently, the police have quelled the riot the usual way. With hoses and billy clubs. "You missed the whole thing," the security guy says. He's right. When we get outside the building, there is little sign of what had occurred earlier, other than numerous red blotches of blood mixed in with the trodden snow.

"And the *Times-Informer* wants an ad praising these people?" Rick says.

-63-

Never before have I been left off the master memo list coming from Quentin in New York, nor have I had to wait on that long line outside his office.

All of a sudden, I'm reduced to peon status, and when I'm summoned down to New York by His Majesty, I must wait and wait some more with all the rest of the beaten-down horde. They snicker at my loss of status, a humbling experience. But in spite of it, I'm feeling pretty cocky today.

Quentin will, of course, know of the glowing memo I received from the CEO of AAB/Worldwide, the super-powerful Max Schaeffer, congratulating me on a stunning show of creativity and profitability in Boston. Quentin was cc:'d on it. So I'm naturally wondering what Quentin is up to. Seems the more accolades I get, the crazier he gets.

When, eventually, the towering Olga allows me to cross the sacred threshold, Quentin doesn't greet me in his usual "big brother" fashion. This is a confirmation that I am now reduced to serfdom, a status I have experienced many times in other jobs just prior to being fired.

Quentin gets right down to it. "I had a call from Lorne Chambers yesterday. He said you refused to cooperate with him and that he had to write an ad for the *Times-Informer* himself."

"That's right, it was a pro-police ad and I wouldn't touch it."

"*You wouldn't touch it?*" Quentin says, accentuating each word. "You just took it upon yourself not to do the ad? Is that what I am hearing?"

"You got it, John," I say, standing my ground. "I took it upon myself not to work on an ad that glorifies a bunch of out-of-control cops who think nothing of beating, maiming, and even killing people."

"To keep law and order!" Quentin sharply interrupts me. "To keep law and order! They have to take care of those rabble-rousers and hoodlums, the druggies and the hippies and subversives that are trying to take over this country. I'd like to see each and every one of them locked up with the key thrown away. If it was up to me, I'd get them off the street and keep them off."

Quentin is raving. I let him rave. "And that includes some of these people in your department, Nelson Banner, for one. According to Lorne, Nelson physically attacked him when he tried to re-direct your approach with Boston National. I agree with Lorne that he should be fired."

"Go ahead and fire him," I say calmly, liking this new, calm Bob Bronson, a Bronson who doesn't throw fits anymore. "He'll just take our very lucrative high-tech clients with him to another agency and it will be our loss."

I can't help thinking that the problems with Nelson and the pro-police ad are just a pretext for the beef Quentin really has with me. He's going nuts because I've had a tiny bit of press attention and that, under my direction, Boston has had a number of entries accepted for the upcoming Magnus Advertising Awards whereas New York didn't get a single entry past the judges--including his New Zealand surrealistic spots.

The way he's acting, I flash back to the down and out-looking guy who was waiting outside AAB headquarters that time. What was his name? Maxwell Baker. He was Quentin's favorite guy up until the time when he wasn't.

Quentin is back to pushing Lorne in my face. "I have to tell you that Lorne didn't have a whole lot of good things to say about you, either," Quentin says.

"What exactly is your point, John?" I ask, waiting for yet another of his verbal blasts.

"My point is that you need to follow Chamber's example of

what it takes to be a good ad man."

"If I followed Lorne Chambers, John, I would be a dou-ble-dealing, back-stabbing, trouble-making asshole."

"That's no way to talk about someone who is helping you prevent clients from jumping ship."

"That's bullshit, John and you know it. We haven't lost a single account since I've been the creative director. If anything, we've had a load of new ones--all impressed with the work we're turn-ing out. We've even managed to hang on to MassAssurance."

I can argue my case further, but why bother? I simply rely upon the Schaeffer memo to keep the balance in this meeting.

Before I leave Quentin's office for the relatively sane world outside his door, he has one other bit of lunacy to express. "I've had a complaint that you and your whole department are looped on drugs."

Considering that this remark is coming from a major al-co-holic who gets shit-faced every lunchtime and every night, I almost laugh out loud.

But instead, I merely face John and look him in the eye before answering.

"Well, as a matter of fact, I shot up on that fucking line outside your door while waiting two hours to see you."

-64-

Once again I've managed to survive another grueling session with John Quentin, but I know it's only a matter of time before he'll think up another weird accusation, one he can try to make stick. I don't have long to wait long. It's exactly a week since John's last attempt, and now he's back at it with something even more bizarre. It turns out that the surrealistic commercials he insisted on making in New Zealand are a total disaster. They haven't increased sales one iota. If anything, the spots are an embarrassment to AAB/New York with the client now looking at other shops.

Unbelievable as it is, Quentin is blaming me for the disaster. You don't have to be a genius to guess what he's up to.

"Whoa, John," I object. "I didn't write or produce those spots. You thought that by making people believe they could buy a product and be transported to some fantasy land, they'd rush right into the paint stores and buy this stuff." I am wasting my breath.

"You must have seen those commercials were really bad and that they weren't going to work," he says, "but you kept your trap shut. I had you with me in New Zealand as a trusted advisor and you didn't advise me. You let me carry on and make a load of shit."

This whole thing is mind-boggling. "No one could have talked you out of making that load of shit," I say. "I tried. You were in love with those commercials. They were your baby."

"If you knew they were lousy, why didn't you speak up?"

Quentin asks.

"Okay, John, You are right," I say. "I should have made my point even clearer that this campaign was one of the worst examples of advertising ever conceived. It was dishonest and just plain demeaning in terms of the consumer's intelligence, and it was apparent from the first that no viewer in his right mind would believe that by using this paint, he would wind up on a glacier in New Zealand."

From the twitches in Quentin's face, I know he would like to fire me on the spot for that statement, but he can't. Schaeffer likes me and I'm considered valuable by the top echelon of the New York management—so I have certain leverage. But he can try to make me quit. When I don't, he looks genuinely puzzled. He's probably thinking: *What's wrong?* According to my reputation, I usually quit at the drop of a hat. Well, the hat has been dropped with a seismic thud and I haven't said a word about walking out.

And the reason I haven't said a word about walking out? It's all about Allie. I want to prove to her I can keep a job even in the worst of situations and that we can start our lives anew. So I don't do my usual thing which is to throw a fit and get the hell out.

Quentin is confused. His plan isn't working. Maybe he thinks I could make a fuss with management. Good, let him think it. It would be very easy to prove the commercials were all his idea.

Then I realize I don't have to prove a thing. He bragged so much about creating the spots, everyone in the New York office knows it.

-65-

If it's not Quentin giving me grief, it's Lorne, and if it's not Lorne, it's Julie. Much as I try to please her, I don't feel any sexual desire for her. Before this, I was able to keep up a masquerade, but any passion that was there is now gone. Zilch. Disappeared. I don't know what happened to it.

She's all soft curves and crevices, and they do nothing for me. Her control issues have dampened my ardor. Julie, on the other hand, has shown no signs of wanting to end the relationship. To the contrary, she's more ardent than ever, more imaginative. It doesn't matter what she does—I've just lost it, and there is nothing I can do about it. If it's gone, it's gone.

To avoid hurting her feelings, I try to hide my lack of sexual feelings for her. You can only do that for so long before it's glaringly out in the open.

"I bet you'd be able to get it up for your wife." She says mockingly. "Maybe we should have her photo by the bed! That might turn you on."

As much as I want to be there for Julie, her mention of my wife is hard to hear because yes, Allie is my wife, and no one can take her place. That fact is more and more clear to me.

It's not fair to Julie, but how do I handle this? I'm afraid if I say something, she'll be bitchier than ever. And I have to keep in mind that she's a sick woman who is going to die. She doesn't need extra grief right now.

I make excuses saying I'm stressed out from work, not that Julie is buying that story.

"You just won't commit to me," Julie says. "You're still married to that woman."

She looks so vulnerable. And her wig is crooked, revealing some hair. I start to straighten it and Julie pulls away.

"What are you doing?" Julie asks, somewhat alarmed.

"I was just straightening out your wig—it's lopsided," I say.

"Sorry," Julie says, "I thought you were trying to remove it. I don't want anyone seeing me bald."

"I've already seen you bald, remember?

One of my weaknesses is that even though I can walk out on jobs, I can't walk out on people in trouble. Look how I got myself into a jam by hiring Lorne. Julie is sick and I need to refrain from anger or impatience when she gets into a mood. I want to be there for her.

-66-

The raid on AAB/Boston occurs after a note, type-written anonymously, has been sent to the Boston police specifying that an ample supply of drugs would be found in the creative department.

I watch as the police search our offices, leaving the rest of the agency strictly alone. Which means that whoever alerted the police made it quite clear where to search. And who else could have sent that note but Lorne, seeking revenge on Nelson and the rest of us.

Police, in crash helmets, order us out of our offices and into the hall, where the search is being conducted. Amy, Sheila, and even my secretary, Sondra, submit by emptying their handbags. As for Julie, today is Friday and she's at the hospital for treatment.

Nikki and her assistant, Rachel, who just happen to be on our floor also get searched. Nelson, Carl, Abraham, Rick, Healy and I comply by emptying our pockets.

Then we're roughly frisked. "Do you now or have you ever possessed any illegal drugs such as marijuana, heroin, LSD, co-caine?" A cop wearing shades asks.

"None of us has to answer that question," I say.

"We'll see if you answer or not," the cop says, his hand on his truncheon.

I repeat what I've said, loud enough so that the writers and art directors hear me. I want to make sure they know their rights are being trampled on.

"I'm going to fix you, motherfucker," the cop with the trun-cheon shouts, moving toward me.

Just before I am sent to never-never land, I hear someone ask: "Do you have a warrant for searching our offices?" It's Shei-la. She's facing down the cop. Carl, astounded as we all are, tries to pull her away, but she shakes him off.

"You have to have a warrant for coming up here," Sheila says. The cop stares at her, unable to adjust to the idea that this dumpy, four foot nothing woman is addressing him like this.

"You're asking for some of the same," the cop says when he finally finds his tongue.

"Go head, you coward, hit me," Sheila says. "But you better hit hard because I'm going to roast your ass over a hot fire the first chance I get. You and these other so-called officers of the law. Ha! There are good cops and we're thankful for them, but you're nothing more than a gang of thugs and it's about time someone put you in your place."

"Okay, bitch, you asked for it." But before he can clobber Sheila over the head, Carl jumps him from behind and has him around the neck. The cop tries to throw him off and Carl hangs on. It's like Carl is riding a wild bronco.

This is when Nelson grabs the fire hydrant off the wall, pulls the lever, and lets the cop have it full in the chest. Rick jumps into the fray along with Healy, Amy, Nikki, and Abraham. I'm not going to stand by and do nothing, so I jump onto one of the other cops and find myself rolling over and over with him on the floor.

But it's no good. They have guns. And when they're out of their holsters and pointed at us, we know we are defeated. We're ordered to stand with our hands on our heads. We watch as the cops rip up the place.

Nikki refuses to obey and is pushed against a wall. Incensed, she goes wild and knees the cop who has pushed her. He falls onto the floor in so much pain he can't even scream, and an-other cop rushes forth to defend his friend from Nikki who has now picked up a heavy, electric typewriter and is about to send it crashing down on the floored cop.

This is officially a police standoff. "One step further and your friend here gets a Remington Speedwriter 520 in the chops," Nikki says.

A cop then points a gun at her and says "drop it."

"Well, if you insist," Nikki says, dropping the typewriter. It misses the prone officer by half an inch.

"Okay slut," the cop with the gun shouts. "I've had it with you." As he takes a step forward, Rachel moves between him and Nikki.

"She was provoked," Rachel screams, outraged.

"Stand over there with the others, bitch," the cop orders.

"Not without her," Rachel insists.

"Handcuff these two whores," the cop orders.

"Watch your language," I say. The cop appears to be deciding who to hit first, Nikki, Rachel or me. I can see how he might confuse Nikki, in her short shorts and 6-inch ankle strap shoes, fishnet stockings, and halter top, with being a hooker.

But Rachel, Nikki's assistant? She dresses like her boss and that's the end of any similarity between the two. With her looks, or lack of them, she would make the homeliest hooker in town.

Just then a cop comes out of Nelson's office holding what looks like a kilo of hash in his big paw. "Whose office is this?" the cop growls. Nobody answers at first, but Nelson's name is right on the door.

"If you could read, you shit-eating worm, you'd know whose office this is," Nelson says. For this, he gets a crack on the head with the stick. He sinks to his knees, instantly unconscious. We stare down at him in disbelief. There's a gentle flow of crimson coming from his left ear.

By the time the ambulance arrives, there are two people ready for stretchers, one of them being the cop Nikki kneed, and the other being Nelson. We watch unbelievingly as he is carried out of the agency.

"Nelson," Nikki screams, attempting to run after the gurney holding him, but her path is barred.

"Move," a voice booms in my ear. A rough shove propels me, along with the others, toward the elevators. I count the survivors—Carl, Sheila Healy, Rick, Amy, Abraham, Nikki, Rachel and a couple of paste-up people from the bullpen.

No sign of Hewitt or Wolfman. I know they're chummy with Lorne—so, who knows, maybe he warned them to avoid the creative department this afternoon.

I doubt that the rest of the agency personnel—the account execs, the media department, the research unit or the production people—have even been called out of their offices, it being obvious that the cops were focused on the creative department alone.

Standing there with what looks like a smile on his face is Lorne. I try to jump out of the formation and land a good one on his obnoxious kisser. For my trouble, I get the barrel of a rifle in the ribs.

When the elevator doors close, fifteen handcuffed detainees ride the forty-one floors down, guarded by four cops, one of whom holds a shotgun on us.

"Move one inch and I'll blow your fucking heads off," he advises us.

-67-

Fingerprinted, photographed, harassed, interrogated and thrown into cells, we have to wait until the next morning to be arraigned.

The charges against us include illegal possession of drugs, assault and battery directed toward the Boston Police Department, resisting arrest, and destroying private property.

The last charge is a laugh considering the mess the cops have made of our offices. During the raid, they slashed the couches, ripped bookcases from the wall, dumped files out of drawers, and even pulled carpeting from the floor.

Other than his name being read off during the arraignment, there is no mention of Nelson or how he came to be bludgeoned, hospitalized, and in a coma. We have no idea as to his condition or if he's even still alive.

Just when we think we're going to spend the rest of our lives in prison, we are released on bail. Each of us is made to cough up a thousand dollars, due within 24 hours. We wait in our cells a further six hours. We're made to understand that we'll have to return and go before a judge when the court can arrange it. Until that happens, we're warned we must remain within a 250-mile radius of Boston.

I calculate that Portsmouth is well within that limit, and so is Manhattan where we're due in a couple of weeks for the Magnus Advertising Awards.

Nikki is sporting a black eye, but otherwise the rest of us are in pretty good shape, taking into consideration everything that has happened.

"Did you have that black eye before you went into your cell?" I ask Nikki, whispering.

"Not exactly," Nikki whispers back, glancing at the Mount Rushmore profiles of two matrons.

I'm wondering when we'll have to return for a court date. According to Barney Rothstein, our newly acquired lawyer, God only knows when that will be.

"You'll be notified of a court date in due course, but that's just for a hearing to determine whether this case should go to trial," Barney says. "The courts are backed up like bad plumbing because of the thousands of protesters out there getting arrested. This could drag on till 1980. Meanwhile, I'm gathering evidence against the cops and how they lost control, and how they sent your friend Nelson Tanner to the hospital with a grave and possibly fatal injury. And aside from anything else, I want to see the note that was allegedly sent to the cops."

"Allegedly?" I ask.

"Yeah. allegedly. The cops have been framing a lot of people recently. They'd like to depopulate Boston of any troublemakers. Your friend, Nelson, was a troublemaker."

"I'd like to see that note, too," I say.

The first thing I do after being released is to head back to the agency. On the elevator, I don't press the button for my floor. I push it for the account executives floor.

There are startled looks on the faces of the people I brush past as I head for Lorne's office. He looks up, also startled. My rage is enormous. I grab him by the lapels and drag him out of his seat.

"You sent that note, you bastard," I say.

"What note? What note? What note?" Lorne is terrified at my rage, a rage he has never witnessed before.

"You wanted to get back at Nelson, so you sent a note to the cops saying there were drugs in the creative department and now Nelson is in a coma. Admit it or I'll break your damn neck.

"I swear it, Bobby, I don't know anything about this. And

what drugs? I don't know anything about any drugs in the creative department."

He can deny it all he likes, but I know he's the rat that got Nelson brained. No one else would have done it.

-68-

The great ad man, Jerry Della Femina once described advertising as "The most fun you can have with your clothes on." Well, we're all fully dressed and no one seems to be having any fun, not since the police raid. Nelson hasn't rallied and we're all just going through our paces, doing our work and banding together like a bunch of survivors from some war-torn country.

I don't know how we're doing it, but we're continuing our output of innovative ads. Not that we're taking much notice, but we have some media and trade journals mentioning us.

In the section titled 'What's New?' in Agency Magazine, our ads share the spotlight with three other agencies this month. It's a start. Featured is the work we've done are for Allied Produce, a company that imports pineapples, apples, bananas and oranges.

The ad for navel oranges reads: *We'd like you to contemplate our navel.* And there's a companion ad showing a bunch of bananas with labels that advertise our oranges. The headline is: *We taught our bananas how to sell oranges.*

Another campaign gaining attention is for our upscale British car account. The first ad reads: *How to say it all without saying a word.* No other copy just a dramatic shot of the car, a sports model. A second ad also without body copy simply reads: *it's made the way they don't make them anymore.* A third ad, this time with copy, shows a royal-looking couple modeled on Princess Margaret of Great Britain and husband Anthony Armstrong-Jones standing next to the car. The headline is: *How to keep up with the Armstrong-Joneses.*

Something that could be exciting occurs when we're approached for a write-up in the advertising column of the *New York Times*. This is a question/answer interview on the state of the ad biz in New England. A reporter from the newspaper is sent to Boston to interview me and some other creative directors from around the New England.

Right before the interview, I get an angry-sounding call from Quentin. "It's not up to you to give interviews," he says. "All such matters must be directed to me." So I direct the *New York Times* to him like he says. They're not interested in him for some reason.

And at that point, I just stay out of it.

-69-

Looks like it's just a matter of time for Nelson. His condition is worsening. A bunch of us are at Mass General visiting him, talking soothingly to his comatose form, encouraging him to get better.

I've heard it said that if a person is in a coma, it doesn't mean he or she can't hear what's going on around them, including the conversations. I can imagine him, trapped that way, unable to communicate, desperate to get on with his life, to shoot up with heroin or to lead a protest. It's an awful thought that gives me a claustrophobic feeling.

His doctors won't tell us anything because we're not relatives, not that any of his actual relatives have shown up. There haven't even been any inquiries as to his condition, according to one of the nurses.

"I called his brother in Brighton," Rick says, outside the room where Nelson can't hear us, a precaution in case he *can* hear.

"He said he had it coming to him."

It's apparent to us, the creative department of AAB/Boston, that we're Nelson's family. Nelson didn't deserve this," Nikki says. Then she begins to cry. Healy puts an arm around her shoulder.

"He'll be okay," Healy says. "It's going to take a lot more than a cop's truncheon to keep old Nelson out of circulation." We're all grateful to hear Healy talking this way, not that anyone believes a word of it.

Nobody believes a word Lorne says, either. He has again denied having anything to do with sending a note to the cops, but we all know he did. He said he would get even with Nelson for threatening to punch him out over the National Bank campaign.

"I'd like to kill the son of a bitch," Rick says.

My thoughts stray to Julie and the fact that it's Friday again, and she's somewhere in this vast hospital, having treatment.

As we leave Nelson, I decide to break a rule of Julie's, which is never to be present when she's at the hospital, but I'm already in the hospital, so maybe she won't be angry if I break that rule just this once and send a message to her as she is undergoing her procedure. I just want to tell her that I'll be in the waiting room when she's ready to leave.

I see Rick and the others off at the front entrance. We all hug and are one in our sorrow over Nelson.

I'll be back in a couple of hours, " I say, feeling such love from and for this small group of people. They're more than co-workers. They're loyal friends. I know that any one of them could leave AAB/Boston for another agency and get more money, but no one has defected. Sheila has had the most offers, none of which, as far as I know, she has entertained.

Walking to the main desk, I ask where Julie Ash is being treated. The attendant asks me what kind of treatment.

"Chemotherapy for leukemia," I say. The attendant spends some time looking through various ledgers and can't find her name in any of them. I'm told that this doesn't mean anything. She says that there are so many new patients that even though she can't find Julie's name, she's sure she's here somewhere.

I tell them that Julie isn't new, that she's been coming here for a while.

"How long?" the nurse asks.

"I don't know," I say, "months."

"For chemotherapy?" the nurse asks, surprised.

"Yeah, a bunch of months."

"No one gets chemotherapy for months," the nurse advises me. "It would kill a person."

"Well, she's been getting chemotherapy for months and isn't dead yet," I say.

The nurse shrugs her shoulders and suggests that I take the elevator up to the third floor and to the radiology lab.

Reaching that floor, I approach the nurse's station and ask if Julie Ash is there and if I can get a message to her. She looks on a roster and reports that she can't find Julie's name.

"She comes here every Friday," I tell her.

"I work in radiology and I would know," the nurse says, "and I don't recall anyone by that name coming for treatment. What does she look like?"

I describe Julie to her, but she looks blank.

"Are you sure she comes to Mass General and not one of the other hospitals?"

She says this while still trying to locate Julie's records. "It doesn't appear that this woman has ever been here," she says finally.

This is unbelievable. I make the nurse look through the files again. The results are the same. No one by the name of Julie Ash has ever received chemotherapy at Mass General Hospital.

I don't get it. Julie's never been treated at Mass General?

What about all those Fridays? And what about her always being so weak after a treatment, and what about all those times I've heard her throwing up in the bathroom?

I'm trying to figure out the best time to talk to Julie about what I found out, and there is no best time.

"I was at Mass General today visiting Nelson," I tell Julie when I've finally worked up my nerve, which is that evening. "He's still in a coma and he may not come out of it. Anyway, while I was there, I thought I would look for you."

"Look for me?" she asks. "At the hospital?"

"Yeah. The desk had no record of you."

"You were checking up on me?"

"Not checking up. I was simply trying to find you. Only you weren't there. And they said you have never been there."

"Of course I've been there. I'm there every Friday."

"Maybe so, but they couldn't find anyone by the name of Julie Ash."

"Of course they couldn't find anyone by the name of Julie Ash," Julie says. "Julie Ash doesn't have chemo on Fridays or any other day," Julie says.

"So you don't really have leukemia?" I say?

"I wish. I use the name Sandhurst when I'm there. That was my ex-husband's name. Why don't you call the hospital and ask them if Julie Sandhurst is a patient?"

It had never occurred to me that Julie would be using a different name.

"Why don't you call them?" she says, all steamed up, handing me the phone.

"Go ahead, she says, "call them, call them, call them," and then she breaks down into heart-wrenching sobs.

Boy, am I a schmuck…

-70-

To make amends to Julie for what was essentially an accusation that she was a liar and a fraud, I take her out to dinner and then she wants to go to bed. She won't understand that I'm not interested in furthering a sexual relationship with her. This makes her furious, something I can't do anything about. I'm glad that at least she's getting the love and admiration of everyone else in the agency.

Everyone else in the agency with the exception, that is, of Nikki Wasserman. While she and I are discussing a series of radio spots for Aunt Ella's Apple Sauce one morning, Julie's name comes up.

"So you think we can record two spots with the money they're giving us for one?" I ask.

"Oh sure," Nikki says mockingly, "and Julie Ash is a real Hungarian countess."

"What does that mean?"

"That means I don't believe that cock-and-bull story of hers for a minute. That chick is about as Hungarian as Sammy Woo down in accounts."

"Okay, what's going on, Nikki. I thought you liked Julie."

"I did like her and then the other day I decided to find out if my hunch was right and said something to her in Hungarian."

"You speak Hungarian?"

"Honey, I *am* Hungarian. I mean Hungarian/American. My grandparents are all from Hungary. They hardly speak a word of English. You want to get through to them, you have to do it in Hungarian."

"So?"

"So this morning, I bump into Julie in the hall and I mention to her, in Hungarian, that I have 10 projects to get together by tomorrow morning. *10 projekt kezuljon fel a holnapra,* I say. She just looks at me like I'm from another planet. Hey," I ask her, didn't you say you were a Hungarian countess?"

"And?"

"She gets all snooty and says she prefers to speak English only, that she's an American now."

"That's probably true."

"Oh give me a break," Nikki says. "If that dame is Hungarian, I'll eat my sarong. There's something fishy going on, Bobby, baby."

-71-

I don't have time to think about Julie being a Hungarian countess or not, nor do I care. And I don't have time to confront her about having worked at Doyle, Dane, Bernbach in New York. According to a copywriter buddy of mine who has worked there since the agency began, there has never been a Julie Ash in the creative department.

"How about Julie Sandhurst?"

"Nobody by that name, either."

Okay, so people pad their resumes all the time. This is apparently what Julie did. But not wanting another showdown, especially after the leukemia accusation. I let it go. I have other problems, big problems. There's a memo from AAB/New York dated December 20^{yh} that lands on my desk.

The subject is the new managing director of AAB/Boston. Headquarters has taken its time with this appointment, but I don't have to read the memo. I know that Tod is the new managing director.

Only it's not Tod.

Lorne, that sleazy bastard, has wrested the title from Tod, the heir apparent. It appears that Lorne has actually uncovered something pretty shady on the part of Tod, and because of it, he has been rewarded with the title General Manager of AAB/Boston.

Looking for something to pin on Tod, Lorne found a beauty. And what he found was that Tod had been letting clients who were special friends of his, skip on production costs.

Lorne has done it again. Having wheedled his way into the accounts department with Tod as his sponsor, he has had no compunction about knifing him in the back, as he did me.

New York, wanting to keep this situation hush-hush has quietly removed Tod, not pressing charges, and has stuck us with a slimy, power-hungry egomaniac as the newly appointed managing director of AAB/Boston. What a Christmas present!

Regardless of this new development, Christmas preparation is underway. Agency personnel exhibit a happy holiday spirit that permeates the various departments. Sondra and the rest of the secretaries have decorated the reception area and halls. There's even snowy weather in keeping with the occasion.

As is traditional in most companies, the yearly Christmas party has been planned and is about to take place in the big boardroom. So is the yearly Christmas address of the managing director.

The staff is feeling the excitement and anticipation of the season. But there's a hush as Lorne enters the room and is about to make an announcement, his first official act since becoming the managing director.

"I want to wish all of you a very, merry Christmas," Lorne says cordially, "and I think this is as good a time as any to inform you we'll be eliminating a number of positions at AAB/Boston and that 20% of you enjoying the festivities with us today, won't be with us after the first of the year."

Why someone hasn't thrown the heavily-spiked fruit punch in Lorne's face is a mystery. I have to put on the reins from doing it myself. Only someone numb to human feelings could make such a statement at such a time. Only the worst human being on this earth could flatten everyone's chances for a pleasant holiday. But there he goes, walking through the room wearing a cheery smile as if he hadn't just destroyed the merry mood, leaving people in a frenzy as to who will comprise that 20%.

On Tuesday, December 24th, the entire agency closes its doors. Work will resume December 26th. I've made plans to spend Christmas Day with the kids, and of course, I am hoping for a replay on the wonderful experience I had with them and Allie on Thanksgiving.

There's difficulty with Julie. She knows I won't ask her to come to New Hampshire and she knows better than to ask. But she's morose and seething with anger. It's scary to see her like this.

The good news is that when I get to Portsmouth, Beryl is not present. I guess her husband in Norfolk couldn't escape to sea and she's with him.

I'm happy to be with Allie and the kids once again. She and I don't discuss the pending divorce. In fact, Allie hasn't taken any further action—at least there haven't been any more letters from her lawyer. Could it be she has changed her mind? I can only hope.

"I've been going to Alcoholics Anonymous," Allie tells me in the car. "The group is helping me get over my addiction."

"There are Alcoholic Anonymous meetings everywhere," I tell her "There's bound to be one in Brookline."

"There might be, but I don't want to leave here and have a relapse. The people in my group have really helped me. I'm not willing to give them up or to risk going back to where I was."

Allie is adamant. One thing I know about her is that when she has made her mind up, it stays made up.

"Okay, Allie," I say. "I want you to have whatever you need to lick this thing. I'll do anything I can to help."

As I say this, I realize I don't really have job security now. Lorne is my sworn enemy and it doesn't look like Quentin is my protector anymore. Getting Allie home and then getting fired again would be the absolute finish of us ever being a family again.

I return to Boston with a heavy heart as the New Year looms ahead. What will it bring?

-72-

Well, the first thing it brings is my break-up with Julie. I can't keep on with this charade any longer. It's not fair to her and it's not fair to me. Julie has become so possessive that I feel like I'm being smothered to death. Her reaction, when I tell her I'm ending the relationship, is as I thought it would be. She has a fit, accusing me of leading her on.

I know it won't matter what I say, so I say nothing. I thought she might have quit the agency, or maybe I *hoped* she would, but no, she hasn't done that, so there's a lot of tension between us at work—and everyone seems to know the reason.

The second thing that happens as the year turns is the news that Abraham has been classified as 1-A for the draft. He's eligible for immediate induction. I wait for him to tell me he's getting ready to report for duty and to be slaughtered in Vietnam, if need be. Instead, I hear him laying into the government. He says that the bastards in Washington can go to hell.

"They want me to fight? I'll give them a fight, all right, but it won't be in no Viet-fucking-Nam. What has happened to the meek, patriotic Abraham who was so willing to die for his country? The answer is Nelson. It's almost as if Abraham has taken up the mantle left vacant by Nelson. He's no longer the shy, cherubic kid that worked for Guy Ridgeley, but someone to be reckoned with.

The way he battled the cops when they raided the creative department sticks in my mind. It's a wonder he wasn't killed. A black man defying white cops can easily wind up on a slab in the morgue.

"So what do you think you'll do?" I ask.

"I don't know, but I can tell you that this is one black dude that's not getting measured for a body bag. If it hadn't been for old Nelson, I would never have seen this war for what it is. A bunch of fat-assed generals demanding we kill the gooks. Well, we black folks are the gooks of America. I'm not going to kill my brother gooks over there."

Young men, black and white, are reacting to the draft like Abraham, with fiery defiance to the enforced servitude. They have none of the patriotic fervor so common during WWII. Those young men (and women) were selfless in their fight against Hitler and Tojo. Today, draft-age youths are, in unprecedented numbers, refusing to take part in what they consider to be a murderous fiasco and the rape of another country.

"Well, anything I can do to help you."

"Hell, man, you're not in such great shape yourself," Abraham says. "Everybody knows that John Quentin is out to get you. And Lorne Chambers is going around saying your days are numbered. How long do you think *you're* gonna last in this job?"

The way things are going, Abraham is probably right. How long will I be in this job? It may not even last till the hearing, the date of which has now been set.

A trial will cause more unfavorable publicity to the agency and Schaeffer, my only ally, might also turn his back on me. Quentin might persuade him that I allowed drugs in the creative department, thereby creating a sordid scene threatening to drive away our current roster of clients as well as any potential new ones.

The fact that drugs were in the creative department before I became the creative director would have no bearing on the case. I would be deemed unworthy of the post of creative director of AAB/Boston, and that would be that.

-73-

On the appointed date at the appointed time, the AAB/Boston desperados, as the local media is calling us, appear in court— Healy, Rick, Carl, Sheila, Abraham, Nikki and me. It wouldn't be far-fetched for us to find ourselves judged as guilty and condemned before the case is even heard.

The only thing stopping that from happening is the monumental effort being made by our lawyer, Barney Rothstein.

I watch Barney in action. He's been hard at work preparing our defense since the raid. A small, balding man, he's physically similar to a comedian I saw on the Tonight Show with Johnny Carson, Woody Allen.

Rothstein's has been an advocate for civil rights most of his career. He's well-known for defending former servicemen unable to adjust to civilian life and in trouble with the law.

We believe in Barney. Without him, extra trumped-up charges would have materialized and we would have been sunk. Due to him, our case against the police is just as strong as theirs is against us.

Visual proof of police brutality has been introduced by Barney, much to the objection of the prosecution, and is allowed by the judge. Narrating the footage is the surgeon attending Nelson. He goes into minute detail explaining the nature of Nelson's injuries.

When the court has viewed Nelson's comatose body on film and heard the surgeon's report, Barney argues, admirably, that our civil rights were violated by certain members of the Boston

Police Department.

He proves, through photographs of the wrecked offices and even Nikki's black eye, and the testimony of five eyewitnesses from other departments who happened to be around the creative department when the scuffle occurred, that the violence was primarily caused by the actions of the Boston Police Department and that we, in the creative department of AAB/Boston, were merely defending ourselves.

Then quite abruptly, there's a whole different kind of energy in the courtroom. There's a flurry of activity on the part of the prosecution. It seems they are endeavoring to cooperate with the defense.

"What's going on?" Rick, on my left, whispers in my ear. Damned if I know. What's apparent is that the proceedings have been interrupted as the prosecution and our lawyer approach the bench for a three-way discussion. It's all very hush-hush and then, out of the blue, the case against us is suddenly dismissed.

It happens so fast, I'm not sure it actually happened. None of us understands what has occurred. Though elated and relieved, I can't figure how such an instantaneous decision was reached. None of us has even been on the stand, but that doesn't seem to matter.

The drug charge is dropped because the drugs were found in Nelson's office—and without Nelson to take responsibility, there is no case. And there's no mention of the "inciting a riot" charge. It doesn't take long for us to realize that the prosecution, on behalf of the Boston Police, would rather forget the whole thing than fight. Our case would be a source of incredible embarrassment to the police force, with a major public outcry following.

"They're running scared," Barney tells me shortly after we're released. "But I'm not through with them. There's going to be an inquest if Nelson dies."

Meanwhile, he's instructed us to say nothing to the group of reporters who swarm us. He says he will make a statement to the press, which he does. There's nothing flattering in his message regarding the Police Department and were it not for his efforts, there could have been an endless span of days or weeks in the courtroom.

There's enormous commotion when we leave the building. Aside from TV cameras and reporters, there's much cheering from the anti-Vietnam War supporters, along with a huge, hippie contingent. They all hold up placards that display just one word: Nelson.

-74-

It's fortunate and somewhat ironic that Abraham, who never has been able to make it to work on time, isn't here when the military police arrive.

Roxanne, our receptionist comes running into the creative department trying to head off the soldiers, but they rush past her, practically knocking her off her feet.

"We're here to apprehend one Abraham Washington and to deliver him to Army Headquarters," the sergeant in charge informs me.

Rick, in my office going over an ad with me addresses him. "What are you doing here searching for Abraham? I would have thought you would be in Vietnam, killing innocent women and children."

The sergeant, used to this kind of reception, hardly takes notice. But I notice. Unlike the general population that condemns men in uniform, I sympathize. At the same time, I don't want them catching Abraham

When the soldiers go about searching the offices and are out of earshot, I call Abraham at home. No answer. The phone just keeps ringing. He'll be on his way here and there's no way to warn him to steer clear of the building. He calls later, after the military police have left empty-handed.

"I was just about entering the building and saw an army van parked in front," he says. "I thought I'd better get my ass out of there."

"Where are you now? Never mind, don't answer that, this

phone could be bugged."

"You're right. I better get off. I'll be in touch," and with that Abraham is gone. Wherever he is and wherever he's heading, he's on the run, a bona fide draft dodger, something he swore not very long ago that he would never be, but it's a lot better than being dragged off by the military and then shipped to either Vietnam or Leavenworth. I bid him a silent farewell knowing that without him and Nelson, things will never be the same around here.

Well, one thing never changes. Quentin has another trick up his sleeve. Since he can't fire me without Schaeffer's endorsement, he calls me with an enticing offer: A $100,000 a year salary. Nobody makes that kind of money other than superstars like himself and the highest-ranked people in management. And all I have to do for it is return to New York and work in the stifling atmosphere of Quentin's creative department, to be directly under his thumb, and to be forced to do the kind of advertising they do down there.

It takes me exactly two seconds to size up the situation, to thank Quentin for his "generous offer," and then to decline it.

-75-

Nikki is missing. She's been gone three days and is not answering the phone. Her assistant, Rachel, has a key to the apartment, so Bruce and I go over there and bang on the door. No response.

For all we know, she might be in there lying dead. There's a rumor that she's been experimenting with LSD. When we enter, the apartment has that look of a place suddenly and haphazardly vacated. Dresser drawers are pulled out, the closet is open, hangers hang without garments.

Nikki is gone, but where did she go?

It's another ten days before I finally get a phone call from her. She's in Toronto. At first I don't get it. "What the hell are you doing in Toronto?" I ask.

But now I hear Abraham's voice in the background shouting "Hi," and it all becomes clear.

"We got out of Boston just in the nick of time. Another few hours and he would have been caught. And by the way, I have some other news for you. Are you sitting down? Abbie and I were married last night."

"Married?" This is a lot of information all at one time.

"Yeah, I wanted the baby to be with his or her father."

"The baby?"

"Abbie, junior, or if it's a girl, Abigail Suzanne. You didn't know, nobody knew, but Abbie and I have been together for quite a while."

She's right. I didn't know, never even suspected. And now I'm trying to picture it. Nikki, an old lady of twenty-nine and

Abraham (Abbie), seven years her junior.

"And guess what else? I found a job with a local TV station. Was here literally five minutes I found it. There's a whole contingent of Americans living in Canada who want no part of the war. Maybe Abbie can get in with an ad agency. Can you write a letter of recommendation? That would be great. We'll probably be here the rest of our lives the way things look."

Nikki has a point. The war appears to be going on and on, and it's more of an embarrassment than ever. The deployment of the U.S. Air Force in an endless deforestation mission has produced the motto: "Only You Can Prevent a Forest." And yet 50% of Americans still want us there, despite the death and destruction.

Lorne Chambers is one of that 50%. Having found out about Abraham and Nikki's defection, he's walking around in the agency pontificating on how people like Abraham should be thrown in jail for life with the key thrown away.

"And that goes for the tramp who helped him." Lorne says in another of his damned meetings he's been calling for all department heads since assuming the position of general manager. "She's a disgrace to the American flag and a traitor to our country." he continues. "Any obstruction to military justice is treason."

"How about I reveal the way you avoided your own military service," I say, wanting to embarrass him in front everyone.

"I was asthmatic," Lorne says

"You were yellow," I reply.

"I was ready to serve our country."

"You were ready to fall on the floor biting the rug if the army was to get hold of you."

Lorne looks totally abashed for a change. When I go back to my office, he follows me.

"Look, Bob, would you please not act so disrespectfully toward me in front of other people? I know you don't respect me though I can't figure out why, but I want to make this job work and if you are always putting me down, it looks bad."

I don't know what to say. Lorne looks so pathetic asking me this. I've been waiting years to hear him to act like a human being, but I don't trust him for an instant.

"And I have to tell you, Bob, that I'm hurt that you accused me of sending that note to the cops about Nelson. Do you really think I could have done such a thing?"

I'm relieved when Sondra interrupts, reminding me of a meeting. Nothing Lorne has said has caused me to change my mind about him. He's still a turd.

-76-

The meeting Sondra reminded me of is with Sheila and Carl and some of the account team, in the boardroom. They're showing me their work on the new Wagner's Ice Cream campaign. Sheila stays long enough to tell me she's not staying. She has to take off on a location shoot in a few minutes.

"The pipsqueak can tell you all about Wagner's," she says, referring to her husband. Since Sheila's meteoritic emergence as the best copywriter at AAB/Boston and possibly one of the best in all of advertising, she has become almost impossible to deal with.

For one thing, she knows how valuable she is to the agency, and doesn't keep it a secret. Her latest ploy is to campaign for a major promotion in the agency, to co-creative director.

"I think such a move would put the agency on the map," she tells me after a series of agency/client victories. My answer is that I'll think about it, but of course there is no way I would give her that power.

"Well, don't think about it too long, if you know what I mean," she says, a veiled threat.

Of course she must be the recipient of job offers, which isn't surprising. I wonder what ever became of the dumpy little Sheila I first knew. Even her appearance has undergone a transformation. No longer dumpy, she hired a private trainer and is now trim and svelte. Her clothes are out of the latest fashion magazines and her hair is styled by the premiere stylist in Boston, Mr. Raymond.

It must be torture for Carl to work with her. Worse, to live with her.

After she takes off, Carl launches into the campaign. In the first ad, he explains how a guy has selfishly finished off every spoonful of Wagner's in the house, leaving not one drop for anyone else. He appears both pleased and unrepentant at the same time.

"The concept is that it's every man for himself when it comes to Wagner's Ice Cream," Carl explains. "You can be as greedy as you want."

In the second ad, a man in pajamas has snuck down to the refrigerator in the middle of the night with one purpose in mind. He sits at the breakfast table with an empty bowl and a devilish expression.

The theme line for the campaign is *I just finished all the Wagner's in the house and I'm glad.*

"This line will be everywhere," an account guy says expansively. "After people see it on billboards and in print ads, it will be on everyone's tongue and in the American jargon. We will own the market."

How about "I just finished my father's $150 scotch and I'm glad," Rick says jokingly while standing in the doorway. He heard Carl presenting the campaign and has come in to give his opinion. It hasn't been asked for, but that doesn't matter. This is our way of working, all of us dropping into each other's offices and saying whatever we like, with no one taking offense.

A team, copywriter and art director, can be coming up with a campaign, and one of us might walk in, have a look at the rough layout and say *"I hate it,"* but give a piece of advice that will make it great.

If you change these two words around," he or she might say, "you'll have a winner."

I loved this way of working when I was a young writer under Jerry Della Femina. He was the most inspirational creative director I was ever lucky enough to work for.

The agency was Delehanty, Kurnit, and Geller on Third Avenue and 49th. It employed such advertising luminaries as Ann Anda, Frank Seibke, Ron Travisano, Frank Fristachi, Helen Nolan, Charlie Ryant and Rick Baxter (a different Rick Baxter), all of them brilliant.

The only problem was that after a dozen highly-successful, award-winning ads, my head started to swell. As a result, my ego got out of shape and control, and when offered a job at twice what I was making with Jerry, I jumped at the chance.

Young and impatient, I gave up the best advertising experience I ever had and have regretted it ever since.

-77-

The Magnus Advertising Awards are early this year. We have thirteen entries competing for gold, silver, and bronze, which are a lot for the amount of time I've been the creative director. We should all be excited, but we're not. Nelson is dying, Julie is sick, Abraham is a draft-dodger, Nikki is gone, and for me the knowledge that Quentin wants me out brings on all the old insecurities I thought were gone for good.

No wonder we're all suffering a contagion of depression and uncertainty. The only two not in our inner circle are Hewitt and Wolfman. Neither of them has anything in the show. They spend most of their time kissing Lorne's ass. And as with Lorne, I'm the one who brought them into the agency.

Amy has been telling me about working with Wolfman. "This guy is a dud. We're working together and I come up with the headline and then the visual, and all he does is sit there and criticize everything I come up with. Then when we're presenting to the client, he takes over and acts like everything is his idea."

We've all had experiences like that, when some creep steals the show. We sit there and boil, but making a fuss is out of the question. Clients don't want to hear that. They want solutions to their problems.

"Maybe we ought to let Hewitt and Wolfman fly down to New York and take all the credit for all our work and let the rest of us skip the whole damn thing," Amy suggests. But on Tuesday, February 17th, we take an early-afternoon shuttle from Logan.

There's been no contact with Quentin since I turned down

his New York offer. He'll get me sooner or later, I know that.

In this year's awards brochure, he's listed as the Keynote speaker. That ought to be interesting.

I haven't had much contact with Julie in recent weeks, but I know she's seething because Sheila is the agency star, not her. Several of the major ABB/Boston entries are hers, including the campaign she worked on with Rick for Papa's Kosher Pickle Relish that's been lauded in the trade press.

The first of that series revolves around a dinner party with everyone being cheerful and having fun even though *The soufflé Sank, the Duck was Dry, and the Peas Were Like Bullets,* or so reads the headline.

Then comes the payoff line: *It Could Have Been a Disaster.* The body copy makes Papa's Pickle Relish the hero that saves the evening.

A second ad features a jilted bride who decides to hold the reception anyway. *The Church was Double-Booked, the Best Man was Late, and the Maid of Honor Ran Off With the Groom,* is the headline, accompanied by the disaster line.

The Awards ceremony being held tonight is, as it is every year, at the Plaza Hotel. I have fond memories of the place. It's where Allie and I spent the first night of our romance, and our honeymoon. It's where we spent weekends, though we lived less than a Manhattan mile away, on East 57th Street.

Tonight, the place is swarming with advertising types, copywriters, art directors, creative directors, producers and agency clientele. Nobody enjoys the glory of a win more than our clients. It's a night out when they can get drunk, make passes at the women, and make even bigger fools of themselves than usual.

A strident, female voice calling my name drowns out all others. I know that voice. I've heard it too many times. It belongs to an art director I once worked with. She rushes over, arms outstretched.

"Bobby," she gushes, her eyes swirling around in their sockets as she surveys every inch of the room. She's on the lookout for anyone who may be looking at *her.* "You're probably interested in what I'm doing these days," she says.

"No, Marcie, I'm not interested in anything you do. You are a horrible person who will do anything to feed your ego. I haven't thought of you once since the last time I had to work with you."

"Well, I'll tell you," she continues, oblivious to what I just said. "I switched from Scali, McCabe, Sloves to work at J. Walter Thompson, where they made me a group head. They told me my work is stunning and you wouldn't believe the money they offered me. I mean gobs and gobs of it. I'm having a wonderful time, really wonderful. Just shot a campaign in Italy! By the way where are you working now?"

"I'm the creative director of a Boston agency," I tell her. She hears *that*, however. "Ewwwww, Boston," she says and immediately disappears into the throng, latching on to someone else. Anyone not working in New York is a leper.

As predicted, Amy wins a gold but it's Sheila's night. She wins three! In comparison, Julie only wins a bronze for the Biggah campaign. Even Abraham (in absentia) does better than Julie, winning a silver for his Iceland campaign including *See Iceland Before it Melts* and *We give honeymooners a lot more to explore than just each other* and a bronze for *All the benefits of up country living and none of the manure.* I wouldn't doubt that he's the first black man to ever win an advertising award.

All chatter stops when the main attraction of the evening appears. John Quentin climbs the stage and stands silently at the podium, looking out over the crowd for the longest time before he decides to start his speech. He's a tall, charismatic movie star-looking guy in a tux with a white scarf around his neck.

I momentarily forget any problems that have arisen between us. If it hadn't been for him I don't know where I would have been tonight, but it wouldn't have been here.

Quentin talks expansively for a full twenty minutes stating that the work we do, so important in the context of how people live, needs to be inherently honest and insightful. I wonder how many of the audience know of his truly awful New Zealand fiasco or of his complete lack in understanding what really makes "inherently honest and insightful" advertising.

Then, as if taking the credit for the work coming out of AAB/ Boston, he mentions how *he* has led the agency to this incredible victory tonight.

No mention of me as the creative director and the man who made all these wins possible. I feel the slight immediately. He has stepped into the limelight and he's not about to share it with anyone; certainly not with me.

-78-

It's the next morning when I've just gotten into the office that Sondra tells me that Quentin is on the phone.

What now, I wonder...some other ploy to get rid of me. Turns out he's warm and friendly, making me even more suspicious. This time I am on my guard.

"Listen, Bob, I'm calling to apologize. Boy, did I mess up last night. I didn't even mention at the awards that you're the guy responsible for all the great work. I couldn't have done a worse job if I'd taken a sledge hammer and smashed our friendship to bits."

Quentin's got his repentant voice in place, all vulnerable and innocent, and I'm supposed to fall for that. "And guess what. I just did an interview on a TV talk show this morning. It was because of the AAB/Boston victory at the Magnus Awards. This was even better than getting a write-up in the Times."

I don't have to wonder if he mentioned my name on the TV talk show. Or my part in the AAB/Boston victory at the Magnus Ad Awards. I know he didn't.

"I'm going to make up for my terrible behavior last night, Bob. You are doing a superb job in Boston, the job you were hired to do."

"Go to hell, John," is on the tip of my tongue and I have to struggle not to say it. I say nothing because I want Allie back.

"Since you won all those awards in New York, Lorne Chambers has done a little focus group this morning amongst the AAB/Boston clients. His aim was to get their appraisals of the creative product done for them. All have unanimously reported how 'Over the moon' they are with your work."

So that's it. The clients are happy with my work and Quentin doesn't want to ruffle client feathers. "And I want you to know that Lorne Chambers appreciates your excellent work as do I."

This is when I have to laugh out loud. "Sorry," I say, still laughing. Quentin can talk all he wants. Tomorrow he'll be back to forcing me out, the poor, sad, pathetic son of a bitch.

I hang up and immediately get another call. It's Amy and she's crying. "Amy, what's the matter?"

Her voice is unsteady. I can tell she's shaking like a leaf and can hardly get the words out. "I found a letter taped to my windshield this morning, a death threat. Someone wants to kill me. It starts out 'Dear Whore' and only gets worse from there. It describes how I'm going to be killed and dismembered."

"Jesus," is all I can say. "Have you called the cops?"

"I went down to the station. They said there isn't anything they can do because there hasn't been a crime yet. There has to be a crime. I have to be found in a dumpster, cut into a hundred pieces."

While Amy speaks, I wonder: Could it be Lorne again? First there was the one sent to the cops that led to the raid. Now there's this one.

Lorne's been pissed off because he wants to control everything in the agency and he can't control anything having to do with Amy or her clients. He tried to crash a meeting Amy was having with one of her clients the week before and was brusquely ejected.

He obviously realizes he is messing with the wrong person. Getting Amy mad is not a good idea. She may appear calm and collected, but she has a good Irish temper and isn't afraid to use it.

"Where are you now?" I ask.

"At my parent's house. I'm afraid to stay in my apartment."

After getting off the phone with Amy, I immediately call Barney Rothstein. When I tell him the about the threat to Amy, he says he's trying to get a copy of the note that Amy found on her windshield to see if there's any link to the note that put Nelson in the hospital."

The way Barney's talks, it sounds like some TV mystery. This isn't the kind of thing that happens in ordinary life.

Barney is back in my office the next day with both documents. I study them and right away notice one thing that ties them to the same person. Then it hits me. I know who that person is.

And it's not Lorne Chambers.

-79-

I see Lorne waiting for an express elevator first thing the next morning and I tell him I know that he didn't write the notes. And even though he owes me a bunch of apologies for all the trouble he has caused me, I find myself apologizing to *him*. I tell him how sorry I am that I thought he was the bastard who sent the notes.

Next thing I know, as we're getting on the elevator, Lorne has tears running down his cheeks. He takes my head in both hands and kisses me hard on the mouth.

"I love you," he says. "I have always loved you. You have saved my life over and over again."

"Cut the crap, Lorne," I say, wiping my mouth.

For a scene like this going on in an express elevator crowded with passengers and with no stops until the fortieth floor, people don't know where to look. They avert their eyes and cock their heads upward as they nervously observe the display that informs them of the floor numbers. They look like they would rather jump down an empty elevator shaft rather than witness anything more between Lorne and me.

"You know, you and I shouldn't be enemies," Lorne says. "We're brothers."

"Hey," I say. "I only said I was sorry for suspecting you. I didn't say I didn't think you weren't a poor excuse for a human being."

Lorne laughs his huge horse-laugh. "That's my buddy," Lorne announces to everybody in the elevator. "He's always kidding.

He and I go way back." He piles out along with a crowd of re-lieved passengers on forty and I continue to forty-one.

I don't know what it is about Lorne and me. If we weren't in this particular situation where we are locking horns all the time, and if he weren't one of the worst people on Earth, we would probably be back where we were before, him simply taking ad-vantage of me, using me whenever possible, ignoring me when I'm in trouble, hating it when something good happened to me.

There are some people who will always be in a person's life, no matter what. Lorne has been in mine since we were teens, and I can't really imagine a time when there won't be a connec-tion of some sort, much as I don't think it would be welcome. It's like we have this agreement that was made before we were even born.

But Lorne, bad as he is, isn't the one who is really on my mind. It's the person who wrote the notes, the first of which led to Nelson's injuries. I am in agony over what I have to do next, but it has to be done.

-80-

Julie looks fresher and more beautiful than ever. She seems to have accepted that our personal relationship is over, but I doubt it was ever as important as was her career in advertising.

She's full of enthusiasm about a campaign. Her eyes light up as she describes the concept, all absorbed with her own cleverness. I let her go on about it, and then I say it, almost unable to get the words out of my mouth.

"It was you."

My heart is pounding and my palms are wet. I'm not ready for what lies ahead.

"It was me what?" Julie says. "What are you talking about?"

"It was you who sent the note to the cops. And it was you who stuck that note on Amy's windshield."

The energy in the room has suddenly shifted. I feel like I'm on a fast moving train I won't be able to get off.

If I thought Julie was going to put up a fight or deny it or plead her innocence, I was wrong.

"How did you know?"

"You should never write hate letters on your office typewriter. I recognized the damaged keys from all the times I've read your copy."

"Hell," Julie laughs, "I knew I should have pieced everything together with words cut out from magazines the way kidnappers do."

"Julie, I don't think you know what you did."

"I know what I did. I was mad. You never committed to me.

I was thrown aside and wanted revenge. So I wrote the note to the cops telling them there were drugs in the agency. I didn't think Nelson would get hurt, but let's face it, he was an accident waiting to happen. If it hadn't been when the cops showed up, it would have been some other time."

"So you think that makes it okay? And you think it was okay to scare Amy half to death telling her she was going to be killed and mutilated?

"Yeah, poor old Amy. She gets a couple of golds and what do I get? A bronze. I'm the best writer in this agency, in this city for that matter, and all I have to show for it is a lousy bronze."

This is like a pulp fiction novel. Julie, a gorgeous sex-kitten psychopath sitting across from me, bright-red lips moving like a vortex, drawing me in.

"Amy was pretty damn decent to you, Julie, with your supposed leukemia. We all were. I did check at Mass General and they never heard of Julie Sandhurst, either."

"Well, in that case," Julie says after a moment, "I guess I can dispense with this now." She removes her wig and I see that her hair has grown back. "You know, wearing that thing every day has given me a scalp condition. I have to use a special, medicated shampoo."

"And what about you being a Hungarian countess? Was that a hoax, too?"

"Hey, you're on a roll uncovering my various peccadillos. It was an amusing little fib. People liked hobnobbing with a countess. You wouldn't believe the number of dinners I've been invited to."

"Well, the masquerade is over, Julie. And so is your job here at AAB."

"Oh, that's just peachy keen, Bob, You're firing me after what I did for you."

"Did for me?" I ask.

"Yeah, did for you. Who do you think saved your job. Who do you think took care of Powell for you?"

I don't believe what she is saying, but the smirk on her face tells me she's not kidding.

"It was the night you stood up to Guy. I knew you were going to be fired the next day. So I had to act that night. I looked in Powell's desk diary and saw that he would be at his club. Well, I was there waiting for him to come out.

"Julie, what you're telling me is that you're a cold-blooded killer. Is there anyone else you've killed?"

"Of course not. What do you take me for, some kind of nut?"

-81-

"You know," Julie says, "you could call the cops," but it would be your word against mine, so I wouldn't bother."

She comes around my side of the desk and leans on the edge. "Listen, Bobby, we don't have to be washed up." She then leans down and places her lips on mine. I get an eerie feeling being kissed by a cold-blooded murderess.

"I still love you," she whispers in my ear. "We can start all over again, forget about Amy, forget about Nelson, forget about Powell."

"It would be hard forgetting about them, Julie. There would always be something to worry about."

"Like what?"

"Like my becoming your next road-kill."

Julie takes her face away from mine, straightens up and laughs scornfully. "Now I wish I had never told you," she says. "You would probably throw it in my face every chance you got...you killed Powell, you killed Powell, and on and on. But you're not really firing me, are you?"

"If you aren't out of here in a half-hour I'm calling security."

"Crap," Julie says, "I was just in the middle of the best campaign I ever came up with."

-82-

Julie is right about it being her word against mine, as I find out from Barney when I call him to tell him the latest. He listens patiently to my incredible tale of murder and mayhem, including the fact that it's Julie's typewriter that was used to write the notes.

Barney tells me there's only my say-so about her murder confession. He also tells me that the most they can get her for is the threatening letter to Amy. Regarding the note to the cops about the drugs, "the cops would probably thank her."

The only thing I can think of is that there's a killer on the loose. I get the creepy feeling she'll be after me next, and there's no one to talk to about it. As Amy found out when she went to the cops with the note, a crime has to have happened before they step in.

I'm thinking about this when Carl comes to see me. He looks terrible. "It's about Sheila," he says.

I say the first thing that comes into my mind. "I hope she's not sick. She has a big presentation tomorrow."

"She's not sick," Carl says. "and she won't be at the presentation tomorrow. She's taken a job down in New York as an associate creative director."

After what Julie has confessed, Sheila's departure is a mere trifle.

"I don't know what happened to her," Carl says. "After all the success she's had here and all the Magnus Ad Awards, it all went to her head. Bunny Berger recruited her, came up with a short list of agencies to choose from. They all wanted her. BBDO, NW Ayer, you name it. She told me I was a loser and that she couldn't wait to get a divorce. But I don't care what she says. I have to get her back."

It's obvious what's coming next. "I wanted to give you a couple of weeks' notice, but look, could I be released right away?"

-83-

Wildfire isn't confined to forests. Things in advertising happen in one fell swoop. The next news of departure comes from Healy and Rick. They've accepted positions as a team at an up-and-coming boutique agency.

"We'd like to stay," Rick says, "but it looks like the beginning of the end here and we can't wait around to see what happens. This is an offer we can't afford to turn down."

"We would never have had this chance of great jobs if it weren't for the ads we did here, thanks to you," Healy adds. "We owe you a huge debt of gratitude for pushing us to do our best work, but we have to go. You were a great creative director, the best we ever had, and you have that to your credit. Too bad you had lousy, back-stabbing, sons of bitches to deal with."

I almost tell them that they are lousy, back-stabbing sons of bitches themselves for walking out on me. Under my creative direction, they compiled quite a stash of great ads for themselves, but what am I going to do, give them a hard time? They're right when they say that it looks like the beginning of the end around here.

There's no doubt about it that for a very short while, we were a sensational creative force and it now feels like a ghost town. It's ironic that all job requisitions are now going directly to Lorne who wouldn't touch them when he was the copy chief, but now studies each one. Hewitt and Wolfman work directly for him, along with the half-dozen other writers and art directors he recruited through Bunny Berger without consulting me; all hacks.

It's only a matter of time before clients start high-tailing it out of here, fed up with the lack of innovation or quality in their advertising.

I'm not sure when I have felt this down, abandoned, and, in general, scared, when Barney calls me to say there's a warrant out for Julie regarding the threatening letter to Amy.

"They're having a helluva time locating her. She vacated her apartment and has disappeared," he says. "She might be trying to skip the country."

The fact that she's gone is hardly a relief to me. She might turn up at my house one dark night, as she did once before.

Only this time it wouldn't be to make love.

-84-

The phone rings at three in the morning and I figure it's probably Quentin calling to beg forgiveness yet again. Only it's not Quentin.

"Do you know where I'm calling from?" Julie asks right off the bat.

"Death row?" I reply.

There's a silence on the other end. And then: "I'll just make believe you didn't say that. It really pisses me off. Do you know what else pisses me off?"

"Julie, just turn yourself in. You need help."

"I'll tell you what really pisses me off," Julie says, ignoring me, "It's not just that you threw me over for your wife, and it's not even your wife. It's the fact that you fired me when I was in the middle of the greatest campaign I ever came up with. A definite, Clio Award-winner!"

I can't even respond to the craziness of this comment.

"Maybe I should tell you that since my campaign will never see the light of day, neither will your little lady."

"What's going on, Julie?" I say, panic suddenly coursing through me.

"I know where she lives because I followed you on Christmas. You didn't know I was following you. I rented a car to make sure, in case you noticed. And I watched through my binoculars as you two were so lovey-dovey. And I just want you to know that while you two were so together, I was there all alone.

"Julie, listen," I say. "I don't know what you are planning, but please think about this. Allie has done nothing to you. I'm the one you have the beef with, remember? I fired you when you were in the middle of one of your best campaigns ever. I was the son-of-a-bitch who threw you aside. Come after me and leave Allie out of it."

"Are you trying to throw me off my target?" Julie says. "You must honestly think I was born yesterday. Okay, off I go to see your little lady. I'll tell her you said goodbye."

Julie hangs up and I'm left holding the receiver as the dial tone comes on and stays on. I don't know what to do. I immediately call Allie but the phone just rings and rings. Finally, Beryl answers.

"Beryl, you've to get Allie and the kids out of the house! They're in danger."

"Listen idiot," Beryl says, obviously angry at having been awakened, "the only danger I can think of is when comes to my dear sister getting back with you again, and that will only happen over my dead body."

"Beryl, you gotta listen to me. Allie's in danger. There's someone, a woman, coming up to kill her." This sounds absolutely nuts, even to my ears.

"Okay, pull the other one," Beryl says.

"I'm telling you the truth."

"Sure you are, dumdum, sure you are."

"Please, Beryl, let me speak to Allie."

"Okay, gotta go now, and I think it's time for you to get back in your padded cell."

"Please, Beryl," and that's all I get out before I'm cut off.

-85-

With a hand I hardly can keep steady, I dial Portsmouth directory assistance and get the telephone number of the police. When the cop on duty answers and I tell him about Julie gunning for Allie, he takes forever getting my name and telephone number and Beryl's address and then he merely says he'll have someone look into it.

"What do you mean you'll have someone look into it?" I shout into the receiver "You've got to get over there now! My wife is in danger. The person after her has already killed one person and caused the death of another."

"As I said," the cop says calmly, "I'll get someone on this. And meanwhile, I think you oughta relax, mister."

It's no use. I've tried everything, and I have no doubt Julie will carry out exactly what she has threatened. I quickly dress and am on the road in minutes.

There's little or no traffic at this time of night as I get on the I-95 and gun the Plymouth up to eighty and then ninety miles an hour. I know I'm not going to have trouble with the cops because everyone speeds on the Interstate. But I could be wrong. Portsmouth is less than sixty miles away and then it's fifty and then it's forty. In regular traffic, it would take an hour and ten minutes.

Pretty soon I'm passing the exits for Lawrence, Lynn, Beverly, Danvers, West Newberry, Newburyport and finally I fly over the New Hampshire state line. That's when my luck runs out and I see the swirling red lights of a cop car behind me. His siren is going full blast.

I am now in a high-speed chase worthy of Steve McQueen, with the Plymouth Satellite doing what it's built for. It leaves the cop car in the dust. The memory comes back of how the cop in New Zealand chased Quentin and me for 160 miles before he caught up.

In no time I'm at the Portsmouth Traffic Circle where I get on Route-One and continue onto Woodbury and Maple, and then, tires screeching, onto Bartlett, left on Islington, and finally left on Brewster where Beryl lives.

When I get to her house, to my surprise and relief, I see the Portsmouth cops have cordoned off the place. They responded to my call after all.

I jump out of my car and run towards the house. A burly cop tries to prevent me from going any further.

And then I see it just inside the front door. A body in the entry way covered by a sheet. A female arm sticking out. A puddle of blood surrounding it.

"Allie!"

PART TWO

-86-

Two days later and I'm sitting in my office, even though it isn't really mine anymore.

Quentin has finally edged me out, convincing the "Powers that be" in New York that it was because of me that Sheila, Carl, Rick and Derek quit, not to mention Ridgeley, Knas, Ferncliff, Santoro, and Phipps. And, oh yes, he even threw in the New Zealand disaster, naming me as the culprit who *came up with* the campaign in the first place. Additionally, how I allowed drugs in the creative department and last, how I brought unfavorable publicity to the agency by getting mixed up in the "sordid" Julie situation.

The ad business has a revolving door. The amazing, though very brief, period when we were the Boston frontrunners of excellent advertising is now history. And I'll be history, too, in just a little while.

Remaining are the bunch of people Lorne has hired, along with Hewitt and Wolfman, who've made themselves a neat little nest here. The last of my people is Amy who has stuck it out with me through thick and thin.

"We don't want to chase you right out," the smug head of personnel had said when he stopped in my office earlier today to inform me that I am now amongst the jobless. "You have till the end of the day to vacate."

I've been given a month's salary in lieu of notice—this being a quick hatchet job. I don't complain. Why bother?

Poor old Lorne. He comes by and bursts into tears. I have to comfort him, telling him it's all right.

"I didn't want you to be fired," he insists between sobs. "It wasn't my idea. I tried to talk Quentin out of it. You have to believe me."

But my mind isn't on Quentin or Lorne or even losing this job that was once so important to me. The events of two nights ago are still with me, the carnage, the blood, the confusion, the blare of the police sirens, the flood lights, the thick fog, and the white sheet with the body under it.

Recalling that scene, I relive how I fought off the cops who were trying to keep me from running to Allie.

It was only after I pulled the sheet back that I got down on my knees to thank God. Staring up at me was Beryl's mostly-destroyed face.

Then I saw Allie and the kids on the other side of the house, aided by a policewoman, and I was running to them, kissing them all a hundred times, a thousand times, crushing them in my arms.

Apparently, Julie rang the doorbell and mistaking Beryl for Allie in the dim light, pulled the trigger of a 38 revolver. Fleeing the scene in her Mercedes, she collided with a truck. Another Raymond Chandler touch. I overheard someone say she never had a chance.

And that was that. I bundled everyone into the Plymouth and took them away from there, took them home to Brookline Village, to safety.

Since then the house has been filled with friends, some I didn't even know we had. They've brought food and flowers and offers of all kinds of help. In the crowd this morning, there was the familiar face of Denise Lawson, still Allie's best friend.

Thinking of my dear, departed sister-in-law, Beryl, I observe that she came between Allie and me in life, and she brought us back together in death. What was it she had said on the phone when I called to have her get Allie out of the house? Something about Allie and me getting back only over her dead body?

Lingering in the back of my brain is a question: How long

will It take for Allie to connect the dots and realize that were it not for me and my connection to Julie that Beryl would still be alive? How long before she accuses me of Beryl's death? It's just a thought, but a troubling one.

I've just about packed up my personal property and am ready to leave AAB/Boston for good when Al Marino, the progress guy, comes bounding into my office out of breath.

"Thank God you're still here. I thought I was outta luck. You gotta sign off on this ad so I can get it in tomorrow's paper on time.

The typewritten piece of copy he's shoving in my face is for the *What you should know about Your Police Department* ad. It's being adapted to a larger size format.

Because of all that has happened here in Boston regarding the cops and what has happened to Nelson, it makes me slightly sick to even look at it.

"You've got the wrong person," I tell Al. "This is Lorne's brainchild. And besides, maybe you haven't heard but I don't work here anymore."

"Yeah, yeah, yeah, I know, but I can't reach Lorne and it can't wait. If I'm gonna get it into tomorrow's early edition, it has to be approved tonight."

"Well, I can't do it," I say firmly.

"Then I'm screwed. I asked Amy earlier but she threw me out of her office. Everybody else is gone for the day, so you have to do it. All you have to do is check for typos and then I can give it to the typesetter. Just do it, okay? Please? As a special favor to me?"

I start to object again when the phone rings. It's Rick. I know what his call is about even before he tells me. "It's Nelson," he says. "He died this afternoon."

I knew this moment was coming but it's still a shock. There was no way he could have survived. Now he's gone. I feel a surge of anger coursing through my veins and grab the ad out of Al's hands.

"Does the client have to okay the changes?"

"Nah, no time for that, but look, you're the creative director, well, the ex-creative director, so if you see something that needs changing, change it, but will you step on it please so we can all go home?"

"Come back in twenty minutes," I tell Al.

Rolling up my proverbial sleeves, I get right to work. I first commend the cops who are dedicated to protecting us. Then I target the rotten ones. I identify and name the ones who raided the agency and killed Nelson. I also name the *Boston Times-Herald* and a dozen other major businesses that have supported police aggression. I even name AAB/Boston. By the time I finish, the copy bears no resemblance to Lorne's original version.

"You got it done?" Al asks when he returns. "I gotta run this over to the typesetter right now so it will be ready for the morning."

For a moment I think he's going to read the new body copy and maybe balk. "What are you kidding me? We can't run this," but he just shoves it in the job envelope and departs. He'll hand the envelope to the typesetter, and then the complete ad will be delivered to the *Times-Herald* by courier and that will be that. I'm thinking how, by tomorrow morning, all hell will break loose.

It's one of the best pieces of copy I have ever written, a true expose, and I relish the thought that the next people to read it, some 245,572 of them, will be the newspaper-buying public.

What I've written is sure to embarrass the *Times-Herald* beyond all proportion. They'll fire the agency right away and persuade other AAB/Boston clients to do likewise.

I can hear Nelson laughing his ass off in the next world.

-87-

I thought that maybe Amy would have come by to say goodbye, but I guess I was wrong. Maybe she feels awkward about it. Or maybe, in the end, she just didn't give a damn. I suddenly get that awful lonesome feeling in the pit of my stomach, one of the worst feelings in the world. Just as I think that, there she is in my office. What's wrong with me thinking she wouldn't bid me farewell?

"I want to tell you what happened today," she says, "but maybe I shouldn't."

"No, tell me."

"Well, it has to do with John Quentin. I had a call from him this afternoon. I couldn't figure out why he was calling me."

"What did he do," I ask, "offer you my job?"

Amy doesn't answer at first. And then she does. "Well, as a matter of fact, he did."

"What did you say?"

"I asked him what the salary was and he said forty. I told him no way. Told him to make it sixty." I look at Amy and realize she is dead serious.

I'm starting to feel a certain degree of resentment rising in me toward her. Here she is ready to step into my shoes and I thought she was my friend.

"So when he agreed to that, I told him I wanted a car laid on me. Not just any car, but a Jaguar E-type. He said okay to that, too."

"Sounds like you've arranged a pretty good deal for yourself," I say, trying to hide my bitterness.

"That's not all. I told him I'd want stocks and options."

"Did he agree to all that, too?"

"You bet."

"When do you start?" I ask.

"That's just it," Amy says. "I don't."

"What do you mean?"

"It's simple. When I got finished making all my demands, and Quentin got finished agreeing to them, I told him to take the job, take the money, and take the E-type…and to shove the whole lot of them up you-know-where. Needless to say, I was canned right then and there. So I'm out of a job, too. I would have come by earlier to say goodbye, but I've been packing."

For a moment I'm stunned by the magnitude of her gesture and ashamed of what I was thinking just a minute before. I always knew she was of the highest quality a person can be, but this almost brings tears to my eyes. What a beautiful, beautiful human being.

"So what do you think you'll be doing, you know, in the future?" Amy asks.

"Dammed if I know."

"Because I have an idea. A pretty good one. Just needs some working out. Maybe you'd be interested in hearing what I have in mind."

"Sure, why not?"

"Well, you know I still have these clients who need a home now that I got myself fired from this place. So I was thinking. You told me once I could start an agency, remember? I wasn't ready then, but I think I am now. I can bring my clients and pitch some new ones, and I'll bet there'll be a bunch from AAB/Boston who would want to come along, too. Thing is, I can't do this on my own. I need a partner."

"You shouldn't have any trouble finding one."

"I already have," Amy says. "I'm looking at him right now."

THE END

I'LL GET RIGHT BACK TO YOU AND OTHER ANNOYANCES

If you live on this planet, this book has happened to you. It's a candid, often poignant, often chilling look at some of the absurdities you face daily.

For example, there's the situation where you woke up in the middle of a colonoscopy and the surgeon told you the pain was in your head! And there's the friend who asks our honest opinion on something, and then never talks to you again after you've given it. As a backdrop, there's a symphony of tuneless, groaning, moaning, screeching—otherwise known as today's music.

Charles takes everyday irritations and infuses them with hilarity. You will identify with them, laugh at them, cringe at them, and maybe even do something about them!

There are those family dynamics that cruelly brand you a "nobody" unless you are a "somebody" (annoying). And restaurant kitchens where you can't see what they might be doing to your food once you've complained about it and sent it back (very annoying). And the waiter who flirts with your date, not to mention the date that flirts back (beyond annoying).

So sit back, read, enjoy, and laugh. You'll live longer. Even with the racket the neighbors are making.

ISBN 9780967979090, ebook ISBN 980918915245

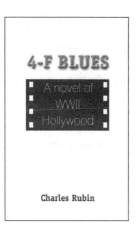

4-F BLUES: A NOVEL OF WWII HOLLYWOOD

The year was 1942, shortly after Pearl Harbor and the film capital was trying to adjust to the blackouts, rationing, and millions of soldiers, sailors and Marines passing through town.

Motion pictures, a powerful aid to the righteous Allied cause, were being turned out by the hundreds.

Studios conducted huge, glittery bond drives while formations of B-24s overhead dipped their wings.

And at the Hollywood Canteen, servicemen about

to be shipped off to such destinations a Guadalcanal were entertained nightly by glamorous movie stars.

In the midst of all this, Hollywood stuntman, Tom Driscoll, classified as 4-F and unable to do what he wanted most—fight for his country—was about to serve his country in a way he never expected.

This is a fascinating story of a Hollywood long gone, when everyone banded against the enemy.

…Almost everybody

PENN Award Winner. ISBN 9780967979007, EBOOK ISBN 9780918915030

This book defies the myth that parents must sacrifice themselves. Instead, it shows them how to reclaim their power, balance, happiness...and lives!

A Guide for Parents of Drug and Alcohol Addicted Children

DON'T LET YOUR KIDS KILL YOU

Charles Rubin

NEW REVISED EDITION

DON'T LET YOUR KIDS KILL YOU: A GUIDE FOR PARENTS OF DRUG AND ALCOHOL ADDICTED CHILDREN

When kids turn to substance abuse, parents also become victims as they watch their children transform into irrational and antisocial individuals.

This harrowing scenario finds parents buckling beneath the stress—often with catastrophic consequences: Divorce, career upsets, breakdowns, even worse.

DON'T LET YOUR KIDS KILL YOU is a landmark work that dares focus on the plight of the confused, distressed parent and not the erring child. It sets aside any preconceived ideas that parents are to blame for what is essentially a full-blown global crisis.

Drawing on interviews with parents who've survived the heartbreak of kids on drugs or who are alcoholic, combined with his own experience, Charles Rubin provides practical advice on how parents can help themselves and their families by first attending to their own needs. Liberation begins when you open this book.

DON'T LET YOUR KIDS KILL YOU: A GUIDE FOR PARENTS OF DRUG AND ALCOHOL ADDICTED CHILDREN has received hundreds of 5-Star reader reviews on Amazon and elsewhere. Such comments as "No other book like it" and "It saved my life' and "A wonderful lifeline just when I needed it" and "Awesome and Inspiring" are just some of those comments. It's the only book on the market that focuses on the recovery of the parent.

ISBN 9780967979038, eBook ISBN 9780987979078